Born in 1911, John Mulgan was educated at Auckland University College where he studied English and Classics, and Merton College, Oxford, where he took a first in English Literature. He worked at the Clarendon Press until the onset of war in 1939, during which time he completed Man Alone, his only novel. Mulgan served with the British Army, initially in the Egyptian desert and later – having quarrelled with his commanding officer – as a member of the SOE, behind enemy lines in Greece. In Cairo, on the evening of Anzac Day 1945, he deliberately took an overdose of morphine.

Peter Whiteford is a Professor of English Literature at Victoria University of Wellington. He has edited the *Selected Poems* of Eileen Duggan, selections of the letters of Ursula Bethell and John Mulgan, Mulgan's war memoir *Report on Experience*, and his previously unpublished *Journey to Oxford*.

The VUP Classics collection
celebrates more than half a century of stellar publishing
at Victoria University of Wellington

The End of the Golden Weather by Bruce Mason *1962*
Ngā Uruora by Geoff Park *1995*
Breakwater by Kate Duignan *2001*
Lifted by Bill Manhire *2005*
Girls High by Barbara Anderson *1990*
Portrait of the Artist's Wife by Barbara Anderson *1992*
Wednesday To Come: Trilogy by Renée *1985, 1986, 1991*
In Fifteen Minutes You Can Say a Lot by Greville Texidor *1987*
Eileen Duggan: Selected Poems edited by Peter Whiteford *1994*
Denis Glover: Selected Poems edited by Bill Manhire *1995*
The Vintner's Luck by Elizabeth Knox *1998*
Man Alone by John Mulgan, edited by Peter Whiteford *1939*

MAN ALONE

John Mulgan

Edited by
Peter Whiteford

Victoria University of Wellington Press

Victoria University of Wellington Press
PO Box 600, Wellington
New Zealand
vup.wgtn.ac.nz

First published 1939 by Selwyn and Blount, London.
No date on title or imprint page.

Subsequent editions:
Hamilton: Paul's Book Arcade, 1949, 1960
Auckland: Longman Paul, 1969, 1972
Auckland: Penguin Books, 1990, 2010

This edition first published 2021
Foreword and textual corrections © Peter Whiteford, 2021

A catalogue record is available from the
National Library of New Zealand.

ISBN 9781776564156

Printed by Markono Print Media Pte Ltd, Singapore

FOREWORD

Peter Whiteford

In August 1936, John Mulgan announced to his parents that he was 'working on a novel which I have about half done – I don't know how it will turn out but I like doing it' (*A Good Mail*, p. 102).[1] There is no further mention of any novel until, almost two and a half years later, he writes to his father: 'You will be pleased to hear that I have sold a novel – a very political novel, I fear . . . I'm not terribly pleased with it – one of these sordid Hemingwayesque sort of books – but I hope to improve it. It's called – at present – "Talking of War"' (p. 147).[2] Rather curiously, the letter includes a detail stating that the novel has been sold 'to Hutchinson's'; in fact, it was another London publisher, Selwyn and Blount, who had been offered the manuscript, and who, after several favourable reader reviews, had agreed to publish it. They asked, however, that Mulgan add some 20,000 works to the narrative, covering the time after Johnson had left New Zealand, and advised against the original title. In its place, they suggested 'A Man Alone', 'Escape from Death' or 'Living Space'.[3]

Whatever Mulgan might have thought of their requirements,

---

1   Mulgan's comments on his writing can be found at several points in *A Good Mail* (Victoria University Press, 2011). Page references in the text here are to these letters. This reference to the novel's genesis considerably pre-dates the timeline proposed by Paul Day, who suggests Mulgan began it in December 1937 (1968, p. 90).

2   As an aside, Mulgan's use of the term 'Hemingwayesque' pre-dates by several years the earliest known usage recorded in the OED.

3   The three suggestions are quoted by Paul Day (1968, p. 92) from a letter from B. H. Kerby to Mulgan.

he accepted the offer to publish readily enough, completing the additional work by June of that year, and opting for 'Man Alone' as the title. However, he did not add anything like the extra 20,000 words that had been requested; the additional material in Part Two and the Epilogue amounts to around five and a half thousand words.

After *Man Alone* was completed, Mulgan seems to have paid it little attention. He mentions it briefly again in letters home, describing himself in one as 'not very satisfied with it, it lacks conviction' (pp. 151–52), and in a later letter he describes the novel as 'honest but dull' (p. 175). He is equally dismissive in a letter to Charles Brasch (August 1940) in which he responds to Brasch's congratulatory note with a very similar appraisal:[4]

> Thank you for your letter with its kind words about my novel. I don't think many people can have read it – it was published at the worst of times – but for people like yourself and James [Bertram] to speak well of it, is the best I could have hoped for. I feel myself that it was formless, unpracticed [sic] and to be honest, a little dull, but I didn't have any sense of affectation in writing it, which was a satisfaction to me.

There are almost no references to the novel after that date. When he does discuss his other writing with Gabrielle, he seems ambivalent about his own ability: 'I know I'm not a great writer. . . . I've very little imaginative ability' (p. 206), but remains committed to the idea of writing something: 'I think I will write one good book some day' (p. 210). Whatever he intends to write (these remarks relate to early drafts of *Report*

4   The letter was written while Mulgan was stationed at Coleraine, Co. Londonderry. The original is held among Brasch's papers in the Hocken Library, Dunedin, MS-0996-003/216.

on Experience), it will not be another novel; fiction has been set aside as decisively as poetry had been some years earlier (see *AGM*, p. 136).

Few readers seem to have regretted his decision not to have pursued the writing of verse, but the reception of *Man Alone* has been markedly different, and there is no little irony that a novel he dismissed in the terms quoted above (while still anticipating the 'one good book') should have become a literary landmark, an iconic work, or a classic of New Zealand literature – even if all such terms, once considered obligatory, are now often sceptically enclosed in inverted commas.

To the misfortune of publishing at the wrong time may be added that of publishing under the wrong title, or at best under his second choice. 'Talking of War' was discouraged by the publishers because of its possible ambiguity 'bearing in mind the fact that Hitler is master of Europe';[5] *Man Alone* has, in its own way, proven to be equally ambiguous – has, as Vincent O'Sullivan remarks, 'at times been remarkably misread' (p. 192). (Misread or not, it hardly needs saying that the title is a much better choice than Selwyn and Blount's other uninspired offerings.)

It is impossible, of course, to unread a title by which the work has been known for 80 years, but attending more closely to Mulgan's initial preference can be revealing. As Bill Manhire notes, 'this phrase – "talking of war" – falls at the very end of the opening paragraph. Had the novel been published with its original title, it would have been impossible to miss the perfect chime of text and title' (p. 152). Manhire continues to suggest a number of ways in which the final title is misleading, and argues, by contrast, that the original

5   Vincent O'Sullivan quotes the phrase from the letter from B. H. Kerby. See *Long Journey to the Border*, p. 191.

casual phrase 'tells us much about the novel's angle of vision
. . . [and] sets the tone for the whole book' (p. 159). Similar
points have been made more recently by Hugh Roberts. One
other observation might be made in this regard: conversation,
however inexpressive it might seem in the novel, is (with few
exceptions) necessarily dialogic. One man alone – to borrow
Hemingway's phrase again – cannot be talking of war in
the sense implied in Mulgan's original title, and there is an
inherent incompatibility between the two titles. Mulgan may
have accepted the change, but he must have realized it was at
some cost, and his preferred title is surely not as 'obscure' or
'odd' as Paul Day suggests (p. 91).

The allusion to Hemingway acquired by the adoption of
the new title has been made much of, but the abandonment
of 'Talking of War' might also have lost an allusion of its
own. Mulgan's Oxford tutor, Edmund Blunden, had written
a much-admired memoir of the First World War under the
title *Undertones of War*. First published in 1928, its success
saw it reprinted several times that year, and republished in
1930, 1935 and 1937. That Mulgan had read and admired
Undertones is clear; he recommended it to his father in a letter
of December 1934, adding that he had written his poem
'Memory' thinking of Blunden's memoir (*AGM*, p. 63).[6] Just
as we find in the novel's Introduction, Blunden's memoir
begins with a preliminary acknowledgement that those who
did not take part in the war are not likely to understand its
narration; its first chapter recalls convalescent soldiers telling
tales in a sequestered and sunny spot and in a later chapter
Blunden recalls being asked: 'Got any peace talk' (p. 13).[7]

6   The poem was published in *New Zealand Best Poems of 1934*, pp. 40–41.
7   For further connections between Mulgan's work and that of Blunden, see
Heidi Thomson.

Stylistically, the two are worlds apart – the idea of 'talking' is much more direct in its implications than 'undertones' (one might say, more outspoken) and at the same time more casual and idiomatic, and there is nothing in Mulgan's gritty and unromantic prose that compares with Blunden – but there are, nevertheless, some interesting points of contact.[8] (That one of Blunden's runners is named Johnson (see p. 103) seems purely coincidental.) Observing those convalescent soldiers, Blunden shares their realization 'that the war would reclaim them, that the war was a jealous war and a long-lasting' (p. 1); the figure of Johnson – damaged by all that had happened to him, incapable of forming anything much more than casual relationships or of taking responsibility for his own actions – illustrates just how long-lasting that claim could be. For when, near the end of Part One, Johnson is advised by Petersen that '[he] ought to think a bit more about [him]self' (p. 197),[9] it is difficult not to feel that for most of the novel he has rarely done anything else.

Mulgan's offhand, Dickensian remark to Brasch, that the novel was 'published at the worst of times', proved to be more telling than he had imagined. Not only did the onset of war affect distribution of the work, but existing stock and plates were also destroyed in London, and no new edition appeared until a decade later, when Paul's Book Arcade (Hamilton) was supported by a grant from the nascent State Literary Fund to reprint the work.[10]

8   Coincidentally, the title of Mulgan's own memoir was changed prior to publication; *Report on Experience* derives from a poem of that name by Edmund Blunden.

9   Quotations from *Man Alone* are from this edition.

10 The grant to Paul's Book Arcade was among the first to receive approval, on March 18, 1948. It would appear that the idea of re-publishing had been in Blackwood Paul's mind for some time. A card to him from Gabrielle Day, dated

Just as telling, but in a different way, was the early review essay by James Bertram, published in *Tomorrow* (May 1940).[11] The connection between Mulgan's title and the ending of Hemingway's *To Have and Have Not* was proposed from very early. Bertram begins his review quoting (or rather misquoting, perhaps from memory) the final words of the central character, Harry Morgan: "One man alone ain't got a bloody f-----g chance" [sic].[12] Hemingway's novel had been published in 1937, by Scribner in New York and by Jonathan Cape in London, and it seems likelier that Mulgan would have read the Cape edition (which omits the expletive). Bertram was unaware that *Man Alone* had not been Mulgan's original choice – that was not made known until Paul Day's 1965 article – and he was equally unaware that the novel was 'about half done' before *To Have and Have Not* was published; he clearly assumed the allusion to Hemingway was deliberate. That assumption no doubt influenced this review, as it did his review of the new edition in 1949. Bertram's emphasis on the 'man alone' motif, together with his account of the novel's 'bare realism', its 'integrity', its 'bare and grim' story, led him to applaud the work as 'one of the strongest and most unsentimental bits of writing these islands have ever produced'. The terms with which he celebrated the novel (he welcomed it as 'a literary portent in a desert of kowhai gold')[13] ensured its initial placement and

December 12, 1946, expresses her regret about some difficulties he had faced, and speculates that Alan Mulgan might be persuaded to take it to the Caxton Press. ATL MS-Papers-5523-14.

11 For Mulgan's response to this review, see *A Good Mail*, pp. 175 and 176.

12 In the text, Morgan, dying and struggling to speak, stammers his way somewhat inarticulately to say 'a man . . . one man alone ain't got. No man alone now. . . . No matter how a man alone ain't got no bloody fucking chance'. The sequence makes Bertram's point even more forcefully.

13 The allusion is to Quentin Pope's infamous anthology (London: J. M. Dent, 1930).

ongoing position 'at the heart of the nationalist canon' and ensured at the same time that 'Mulgan's position as a distinctly nationalist writer . . . remained a constant' (Murray, *Never a Soul*, p. 199). The problems arising from that positioning (indeed, it might be better described as an appropriation), and the not infrequent conflation of author and novel that seems to be part of the same attitude, are explored further in Murray's book.

In *Picking Up the Traces*, Lawrence Jones quotes briefly from a review of Nelle Scanlan's *Pencarrow* in the second number of *Phoenix*: 'we have the need of the novelist in our midst, but it must be the good novelist' (p. 26). The 'we' no doubt refers generally to New Zealand or the New Zealand literary community, but it unwittingly highlights at the same time the need felt by those of the *Phoenix* group in particular to have prose writers to balance the poets – an imperative that Murray sees as underlying the ways in which Bertram and Day have written about *Man Alone* (p. 200). It was necessary for their purposes that the novel be seen as rejecting all that the previous generation of prose writers stood for (just as had been effected by and for the poets), and this seems to have coloured in particular Paul Day's sense of Mulgan's disdain for and rejection of the work of his own father. He undoubtedly had a very different taste from Alan and saw his stylistic limitations, and he chaffed at having to undertake the role of agent and promoter for his father's manuscripts, but the evidence for disdain or outright rejection is not as compelling as Day suggests.

If the title of the novel has been frequently 'misread', it is equally true that the novel itself has been frequently re-read, in the sense that it has been subject to interpretation from a variety of perspectives, and through a variety of critical lenses.

Many of those re-readings are, to a greater or lesser degree, reactions to the placement of *Man Alone* at the centre of the nationalist canon, challenges to the notion of a canon and in particular a nationalist canon, and responses to the twin efforts to emphasize both its realism and its mythic qualities. At the end of his first review, Bertram reflects: 'Here, at any rate, is one novel that tells the truth about New Zealand' (p. 407). Bertram was too astute a critic to confuse sociological or historical truth with the truth of fiction, but others subsequently have not always preserved that distinction; nor have they always given sufficient weight to Johnson as a fallible narrator. The belief so prominent in the nationalist narrative, that Mulgan's novel was a particularly truthful account of the land and the people he described, remains something of a critical touchstone.

Bertram was right, though, to see it as a novel that would last – or as Trixie Te Arama Menzies phrased it in the title of her article – to see John Mulgan as a man not to be killed. While the novel may have disappeared from secondary school and university reading lists where its presence once seemed *de rigueur*, it continues to receive significant critical attention in accounts of the establishment of a New Zealand literary culture.

That these different critical lenses – Marxist, feminist, indigenous, post-colonial among others – call into question (or seek to confirm) the degree to which the novel can be said to be 'telling the truth' was noted by Patrick Evans in his Foreword to the most recent Penguin edition of the book (1990). He challenges the notion that *Man Alone* is a work of realism, believing that viewpoint to be the product of conscious mythmaking by the *Phoenix* generation. Further, he goes beyond Paul Day's 'version of Harold Bloom's theory' to suggest that the novel is much more than a rejection of parental influence but rather represents 'a brutal and ruthless attempt to stamp out something (we will never know what it was)' (n.p.). It is unfortunate that Evans is unable to identify Mulgan's target; had he done so we might be better placed to assess both his argument and Mulgan's brutality. As it stands, though, the word 'tendentious' seems better applied to his Foreword than to the novel, whether it be considered a work of realism or a romance.

'Because of [a] radical change of sensibility', Evans writes, *'Man Alone* has to be reissued on different terms from before' (n.p.).[14] His reissue presents the novel with a new critical introduction, but it does not otherwise change the text, which is reproduced exactly from the earlier New Zealand editions.[15] And that observation brings us to the final point – that the text of the editions produced in New Zealand is not the text that John Mulgan presented to his publishers or that Selwyn and Blount released in 1939.

The destruction of the original plates necessitated that the book be reset when, in 1948, Blackwood and Janet Paul began to prepare the text for publication. Given that the work had to be reset from scratch, an opportunity was taken to correct some (but not all) of the typographical errors that existed in the 1939 edition, to impose a different house style in terms of punctuation and to modernize Mulgan's hyphenation practice. Regrettably, new errors were introduced, and at the same time a number of textual changes were made that one imagines were seen as improvements to the text.

14 Stuart Murray's review, however, suggests it is a reissue on the same rather limited and limiting terms.
15 In fact, an error crept into the 1960 edition (printed in Great Britain) involving the transposition of two whole lines at the top of p. 141. The error was corrected in the 1972 edition.

Just as the text of *Report on Experience* had been 'improved' by unknown hands, so too *Man Alone* has been changed in ways that Mulgan himself could neither have authored nor authorized.[16] Nothing extant in his papers or those of the publishers discusses those alterations, and it is impossible now to determine with any certainty who was responsible for making them, or for approving them. In this edition, I have restored Mulgan's original readings (except those obvious errors), indicating in the footnotes the readings of subsequent editions. Corrections of literals and changes to punctuation have not been recorded.

In some cases, the changes appear to have substituted more predictable or easier readings – 'impassable' for 'unpassable' and 'clay bank' for 'clay break', for example – and these were no doubt seen as corrections, although both original readings can be defended, and even preferred. Occasionally, other changes that might also have been thought of as corrections have had the effect of diluting the spoken idiom of Scotty, Robertson or Stenning.

The majority of the changes consist of quite minor alterations of wording, but they do have a subtle impact where they occur, even when as minor as a change of article. For example, Mulgan describes Johnson as kissing Mabel 'in the back of a car' which in the later editions appears as 'in the back of the car'. The latter suggests the car belonged to Johnson or to Mabel; the former suggests an opportunistic use of any unlocked vehicle. When Johnson and Scotty leave Blakeway's, Mulgan writes 'There were few farms and they met no one'; this becomes 'There were a few farms and they met no one'. Mulgan's wording suggests a greater degree of remoteness and

16 The editorial changes in *Report on Experience* can be seen in the new edition published in 2010; see the account of the textual history, pp. 17–28.

isolation (and is grammatically better).

Another small change at the end of the novel is also worth noting: Part Two begins with a reflection on the changes that Johnson had undergone in his life, all expressed in terms of what he was not, rather than what he had become. Near the end of the paragraph, he is distinguished from one of his earlier selves, from 'that other man knowing hardship and fear of the future and death by poverty as old friends'. Except that Mulgan did not write 'as old friends' but 'of old friends'. There is no plaintive personification in the lines, no faintly elegiac note, just a final comment on the grim reality of the Depression.

The first New Zealand edition has a brief note on the imprint page which reads 'Three slight alterations have been made to the text of this edition in the interests of geographical consistency; these are on pages 22, 23 and 25'. No reference is made to any of the other numerous changes that have been made, and even that cursory acknowledgement has been dropped from subsequent editions. The material that has been removed relates to the location of Thompson's farm. When Scotty tries to interest Johnson in moving there, he expressly locates it near Pirongia. The name occurs three times within a few pages, suggesting that Mulgan has been quite deliberate in his intention to include it, but since 1949 it has been removed from the novel entirely.[17] No further detail is provided as to why this is considered inconsistent, and if anything I would suggest the inaccuracy may be temporal rather than geographical. Johnson and Scotty are said to have left Huntly and 'ridden all morning' before climbing 'out of the Waikato Valley and the dairy country into the fern foot-hills of Pirongia (p. 41). The

---

17 Mulgan knew Pirongia well; it was where Mary and Walter Scott had their farm. See *Long Journey*, p. 28 and passim.

distance between Huntly and Pirongia is around 60km (rather than the thirty miles Thompson claims), suggesting a ride rather longer than half a day. Geographical consistency seems a rather arbitrary criterion to apply on this single occasion, so I have allowed Pirongia to return.

Stuart Murray's review referred to above concludes with an observation that the 'circumstances behind the writing of *Man Alone* . . . leave it disjointed and loose' (p. 128). Similar points have been made by others who recognize the haste with which it appears to have been finished. Such comments seem predicated on Paul Day's suggested dates of composition (repeated at the beginning of Patrick Evans's introductory note), but the genesis of the novel was longer than they realized, and the looseness of construction really only applies to the added material. But as Murray goes on to note 'it deserves a place in modern New Zealand' (p. 128). That has been the recurrent theme of those who have written about it, ever since Bertram lamented that it had 'attracted far too little attention as yet in his own country' (p. 404). In the intervening years it has attracted considerably more attention, and a greater recognition of its complex place within the body of New Zealand fiction. Whatever judgements are made of it, Mulgan's own self-deprecating comments scarcely offer the final word.

WORKS CITED

Mulgan, John. 'Memory.' *New Zealand Best Poems of 1934*. Chosen by C. A. Marris, Harry H. Tombs, 1934, pp. 40–41.
— . *Report on Experience*. Edited by Peter Whiteford, Frontline Books, Victoria University Press, and Naval Institute Press, 2010.
— . *A Good Mail: Letters of John Mulgan*. Selected and edited by Peter Whiteford, Victoria University Press, 2011.

Bertram, James. 'Between Two Wars: An Outstanding New Zealand Novel.' [Review] *Tomorrow* 6, no. 13, 1 May 1949, pp. 404–407.

— . Review of *Man Alone*. *NZ Listener* 21, No. 531 (26 August, 1949), pp. 16–18.

Blunden, Edmund. *Undertones of War*. Cobden-Sanderson, 1928, 2nd ed., 1930.

— . 'Report on Experience.' *Selected Poems*. Edited Robyn Marsack, Carcanet Press, 1982, p. 67.

Day, Paul. 'Mulgan's *Man Alone*.' *Comment* 24, Aug. 1965, pp. 15–22.

— . *John Mulgan*. Twayne Publishers, 1968.

Hemingway, Ernest. *To Have and Have Not*. New York: Scribner, 1937; London: Jonathan Cape, 1937.

Jones, Lawrence. *Picking Up the Traces: The Making of a New Zealand Literary Culture 1932–1945*. Victoria University Press, 2003.

Manhire, Bill. 'Talking Points: A Note on *Man Alone*.' *Still Shines When You Think of It: A Festschrift for Vincent O'Sullivan*. Edited by Bill Manhire and Peter Whiteford, Victoria University Press, 2007, pp. 152–160.

Menzies, Trixie Te Arama. 'John Mulgan: A Man You Can't Kill.' *Journal of New Zealand Literature*, no. 8, 1990, pp. 74–86.

Murray, Stuart. 'Textual Survival.' [Rev. *Man Alone*, Penguin, 1990.] *CRNLE Reviews Journal*, 1, 1993, pp. 126–129.

— . *Never a Soul at Home: New Zealand Literary Nationalism and the 1930s*. Victoria University Press, 1998.

O'Sullivan, Vincent. *Long Journey to the Border. A Life of John Mulgan*. 2nd ed., Bridget Williams Books, 2011.

Roberts, Hugh. 'Talking of War.' [Review of *Mulgan*, Noel Shepherd.] *New Zealand Review of Books*, vol. 27, no. 4, 2017, https://nzbooks.org.nz/2017/literature/talking-of-war-hugh-roberts/

Thomson, Heidi. '"Poets Had Moved in This Country Once": John Mulgan and Romantic Poetry.' *Journal of New Zealand Studies*, 21, 2015, pp. 13–18.

ACKNOWLEDGEMENTS

My initial work on John Mulgan began some years ago at the suggestion of Vincent O'Sullivan, and I continue to be very much in his debt for his ongoing interest and support. I am equally indebted to Richard Mulgan, who has been generously supportive of these several projects.

I am very pleased to be able to record my gratitude to two exemplary research assistants, Anna Plumridge and Theresa Ulmer, for their invaluable work (some of it many years ago), and to the Faculty of Humanities and Social Sciences for research grants to enable me to employ them. I am also grateful for the period of research leave that allowed me to focus on this project.

I am indebted to staff in the National Library and the Alexander Turnbull Library (custodians of the Mulgan papers) for much assistance, and to staff in my own library at Victoria University of Wellington.

I mentioned the idea of this revised edition of Man Alone some years ago now to Fergus Barrowman, and he has remained enthusiastic through a long period when other responsibilities prevented me undertaking any research. I'm very grateful for that enthusiasm, and the lack of any pressure.

As ever, I am pleased to note the very supportive environment of the English literature programme at Victoria. Whatever the challenges faced within the tertiary sector, these colleagues continue to affirm that our shared work is of value, and continue to create a place and an atmosphere that facilitates research.

Of course, that research does not take place solely in the work environment, and I could not have completed this endeavour without the continued warm and loving support I have received at home.

MAN ALONE

INTRODUCTION

I met Johnson on the quay at one of those fishing villages in Brittany which everybody paints, and got into conversation with him, first of all, because we both spoke English, and afterwards, because we found that we both came from the same country, which was not England. We talked a little there, watching the blue nets of the fishing boats hanging in the sun to dry, and the red dungarees of sailors and the brown-red canvas of sails and feeling over it all the strong smell of fish. Afterwards we went up together and had a meal in the Café de Bordeaux. The café was very crowded with a party that had come in from somewhere in a bus. They took up the whole of the café except one or two tables at the side so that it was difficult to get service or to hear what anyone said, but we were not in a hurry and sat there eating prawns and drinking cheap red wine, and after a while we got to talking of war.

This Johnson, if I might describe him, had just come out of Spain. This was a year or two ago now, it belonged to a different time. He was on leave and was going back again when his leave was over. He was a medium-sized man, very brown, almost black from the sun, with a round, ordinary-looking face and a large mouth and strong teeth stained yellow with tobacco. He had fair hair and no hat, and eyes that were either grey or green. Now I was interested in this war and, indeed, in any war, and I tried to get him to talk about it, but he wouldn't talk much. He said:

"There's a hell of a lot too much talk about war."

I waited a while. The noise in the café got worse if anything. They took away our prawns and brought veal and another bottle of wine.

"You can see war any time you want to," Johnson said. "There's a lot of war about in the world to-day. A few years ago now, it was different. Then it was an old man's story. It was the sort of thing you'd sit around the fire and tell stories about."

"You were in the Great War," I said. "Tell me about that."

"I've been in all the wars," Johnson said, "but I couldn't tell you anything about it."

"You won't talk about it?"

"I couldn't tell you anything even if I did. It wasn't anything. You wouldn't understand it unless you saw it. If you did see it, you wouldn't understand it."

It was very hot and stifling in the café, though as we sat there it began to grow quieter, and the smell of fish and cooking-oil was mixed with tobacco smoke.

"I couldn't tell you about the war," Johnson said. "It wasn't a lot different from anything else. I could tell you worse things about the peace."

"What was the peace?"

"That was the bit in between."

"Worse things?"

"Truer things."

And so I said to him, not wanting to move and quite ready to listen: "Tell me about the peace then."

PART ONE

CHAPTER I

Johnson went to New Zealand after the war because men he had met in France had talked of it as a pleasant and well-to-do country. He had been billeted with some New Zealanders in a rest-camp and the way they talked about it made it seem like the only country in the world. In that period, just at the end of the war, the distance and strangeness that such a journey involved and going there to a new country with no money, was slight beside everything else that had happened to him in the last four years of his life. He was demobilized early and sailed in March 1919 with an 'assisted emigrant's' ticket. The ship that he sailed on carried convalescent soldiers and emigrating Englishmen with their children and families. Four people died on the voyage, two from pneumonic influenza, one armless soldier from wasting and blood-poison, and one old lady from heart failure in the heat near Panama, so that funeral services at intervals regulated the conduct of the ship. A stale tiredness hung over everyone and made the voyage long and wearying. It lasted six weeks, but they came in early one morning to Auckland, and when Johnson came on deck he could see the new country that he had chosen to live in.

What he saw then was the brightness of red iron roofs straggling down to the shore on two sides of a land-locked harbour and clustered together on one side the steel-grey cranes and advertisement-plastered buildings of the port and city. The ship moved slowly in and hung at anchor in the stream while the long business of medical inspection went on. Johnson leant on the rail, watching the shore and the small boats that went by. The deck was full of luggage and people moving and talking. Beside Johnson, a returning New Zealand soldier, still in uniform, spat carelessly into the water. The tide from the upper harbour moved swiftly down tugging at the ship. The warm mist of a day's rain that had lifted hung over them. The soldier turned and said to him:

"That's Auckland, mate—the Queen of the North."

"The what?"

"The Queen of the North. That's what they call it—in Auckland. This is God's own, this country."

"It looks all right."

"It's not a bad little town—nor a bad little country neither. It looks small after London though, don't it, mate? It looks different now to me to what it did."

The soldier had a face that was shrunken and pock-marked and unhealthy-looking; his left arm had not recovered from a shrapnel wound; he carried it stiffly in front of him. He said:

"It's three years since I seen those wharves. We was billeted in the wharf-sheds two nights before we sailed. It was cold as death."

"I didn't think it was ever cold here," Johnson said.

"It's cold enough sometimes in winter, mate, if you're not sleeping in your bed, and we weren't sleeping in our beds."

He coughed, lighting a cigarette.

"It's home again now for me, mate," he said, "and there'll be the wife and kids and all there waiting to meet us."

He spoke without enthusiasm. Johnson said, not answering him:

"D'you know anywhere to stay in town for a night or two?"

"Why, you stay at the 'National'," the soldier said, "right at the bottom of the street." His face lit up. "I used to know the fellows there, if they haven't changed. Jack Oakley keeps it. I tell you what, son, we'll go along there first and get you fixed up."

"You'll have people meeting you," Johnson said.

"That's right, but they won't mind waiting. The 'National's' just across from the wharf. We'll do that and have a drink. I won't probably be seeing fellows like you again for a time."

"Well, thanks, then," Johnson said. "We'll do that then. I'll be staying here a day or two to look about me."

"That's right, that's the thing to do," the soldier said. "It's a nice little country when you know it."

So they sat all afternoon with two other men from the ship at a little table in the long bar of the 'National' and talked, drinking beer. They talked mostly about the war and places they had been to like men that had come back from a long journey that was over now. They talked on quietly and drank beer that was bitter and strong, tasting of tobacco and salt. One or two men that the other three knew came in and, seeing them, walked over to shake them by the hand and to have a drink. But no one got merry with the drinking. There was a quietness and sickness over everything and over the other men in the bar. The men who had stayed there and who welcomed them now, coming back, did not want to hear about the war any more. The men who had come back had returned from another world which they were too tired to describe.

Johnson felt out of things and withdrawn from them, not speaking quite as they did nor having the same background of friends to draw on, but they were very friendly to him. He was young then, not more than twenty-two, and thin and white with three years of war and travelling emigrant class through the tropics. His hair was brushed smooth, his teeth were white, his hands clean, and clothes neat. He did not talk much and spoke, when he did, precisely and like an Englishman, but the others treated him as one of them and called him 'chum' and each bought drinks in turn until the bar had filled up towards six o'clock and closing time. The room was more noisy then, but not more cheerful. It was full of men talking loudly, but no one was listening to what they said. In the end they all went off and left Johnson there. He went up to his room and had a bath and ate dinner almost alone in a large room with a fat, white-faced, dark-haired waitress to serve him. She would not smile at him, but served him, resenting him and the work he caused her. He was lonely then and disliking the strangeness of a new town. Sitting in the lounge afterwards, he read the evening paper, going through the column of 'situations vacant', idly, and not so much looking for a job as trying to see what sort of jobs men were offered in this country.

There were a lot of jobs, jobs of all kinds for young men in offices, school-teachers, married men with families for share-milking, jobs for cow-hands, shepherds, drivers, laundry-men, mechanics, jobs for men with experience, without experience, two pounds a week and all found, small capital will buy share in land agent and stock-broker, old-established, farms well stocked near road and rail, good milkers, on easy mortgage, on small down payment, salesmen able drive, new Ford, old Buick. Beside these were other columns, jobs wanted, situations desired, returned soldier, in good health, soldier's widow, three children for house-keeping, in good health. He read up one column and down another.

While he was doing this there were two men talking on a sofa opposite to him, and he watched them, trying to estimate them, listening to what they said.

One of these men was red-faced and strong looking; he wore leather leggings and a check coat. He was talking loudly and he was saying to the other man who listened to him, tiredly and not speaking—he was younger, this other man, but more dispirited. He had a face that was lined with trouble and a twisted, drooping mouth—and the first man was saying:

"Sam, boy, it's a scandal. It's a graft and bloody murder and I don't care who hears me say it. The whole country's crazy and it'll be years before they see sense again."

The younger man nodded.

"They'll see sense," he said.

"Forty pounds the acre! Sam, you could get land ten miles out of London for less than that."

"That's right."

"And pumice land—it's not farming land—it never was farming land. It's a hold-up, and God help the poor bastards who have to take it at that price and try to farm it."

"They don't know any better," Sam said.

"They'll know better. They'll know better than to think butter'll always be half a crown the pound. They'll know better when the soft stay-at-homes that sold it to them are riding round in cars in town and they're out on their arses trying to pay the mortgage off."

The big man took a pull at his whisky and soda.

"It makes me God damn sick, Sam," he said, "the boys coming home to a country like this and being treated that way. By God, it makes me sick."

When the big man had gone off, the hotel-keeper leaned out across the cash-desk.

"Tom isn't feeling so good," he said.

The younger man's face screwed into a smile, tiredly and dispassionately.

"He's been in town all day," he said, "trying to sell some land to the board and they wouldn't look at it. He's a bit upset," and they both grinned.

"That's a good one on old Tom," the hotel-keeper said.

Johnson went out after that into the main street of the town. There was a fine mist falling that muddied the streets and the pavements. Few people were about in the streets though the shop windows were all lighted up and the picture theatres were open. There was an electric light sign of a kettle pouring tea at the bottom of the street, like a detached fragment of Piccadilly. Johnson walked up the street and down it again. Coming back there was a woman on a corner whom he had passed and noticed on the way up. Now she looked at him and smiled and he stopped to speak to her. He talked to her in the only way that he knew.

"Come and have a drink," he said.

"I could do with one. It's a wet night," she said, "and cold, too. Where'll we go?"

"Anywhere," Johnson said. "I don't mind."

She smiled again. She had a bright red hat and false teeth that fitted unnaturally. Her face was pleasant and kindly.

"You're just out," she said. "There's nowhere open after six here."

"That's all right. I'm staying at a hotel."

"Which hotel?"

"The 'National'."

"I don't think I'll go there," she said.

"What's wrong with it?"

"There's nothing wrong with the 'National', only I don't like it much. There's only one place I know to get a drink."

"Let's go there then."

They turned up a side street running steeply up a hill. She took his arm.

"It's got quieter than ever in this town since the boys came back," she said.

They went in through the swing door of a hotel. The door from the hall into the bar was shut, but she turned the handle and opened it, and they went downstairs into a bar[1] that was crowded with men. There were two other women there who called out to her as she came in. A small, dark-haired boy, with the kind of sharp face that is given to boxers and jockeys and wearing a bright-blue polo sweater, was serving drinks. He was busy, not talking, banging glasses down on the counter as he filled them. The air was thick and heavy with tobacco and the stale smell of drink. Johnson bought drinks and they sat down. He was sleepy then with the drink and the heaviness of the air. After a time, the woman was talking to someone at the bar and he did not mind this and drank his beer and after that two men were talking to him. They were sitting one on either side of him and buying drinks for the three.

"It's a homey," said one of them. "Ah, chum," he said, in exaggerated north-country, "tha-a-at's reet."

Johnson grinned. He did not mind them.

"It's a homey," the other said to the room at large, and clapped him on the back. "Ha' ye just coom over on the boat, lad?" and they both laughed.

Johnson bought drinks for the three of them. One of them was saying:

"I wouldn't touch our Rose, lad."

"She's no good?"

"She's no good to touch."

"I won't touch her."

"He's a smart lad, eh?" one said to the other.

"He's smart all right."

"Listen, you don't want to buy a farm, son?"

1   a bar] the bar

"I haven't got the money."

"You don't need much money. Just a bit down. I could put you in the way of a good bit of dairy land."

"He could do that," the other said.

"I haven't the money," Johnson said. "I'm not looking to buy a farm. I'm looking for a job."

"You haven't got two hundred pounds?"

"I haven't got twenty pounds."

"You can't buy a farm with under twenty pounds—not these days," the first one said.

"I wasn't expecting to buy a farm anyway," Johnson said.

"It's a pity, son," the first man said.

"I don't mind saying you're not right," the other said. "It's a bad time to be buying farms. Prices are crazy."

"I'll tell you something," the first man said. "He's a good kid, I'll tell you something. Don't you buy anything in this country, see, don't you buy nothing."

"That's right," said the other.

"You take wages, son, and you hang on to 'em. I wouldn't say this to everyone, but you're a good kid and you haven't no money."

"Drink up," said the other man.

"I'll buy these," Johnson said, finishing his drink. He put his hand into his hip pocket and brought out a pound note. The first man put his hand on Johnson's.

"You stick to your money, son," he said. "We'll buy these. You're a good kid." He got up and went to the bar and came back with three glasses. They drank up slowly. Johnson was feeling a little sick, but more with the heaviness of tobacco smoke than the drink.

The bar-room was growing emptier by then. Rose had gone. The boy behind the bar was mopping down the counter, whistling through his teeth. They had a last drink, standing up at the bar. In the end they went with Johnson down to his hotel and saw him inside.

"So long, chum," they said. "You keep looking for work."

He shook hands with them both and went inside and upstairs to bed.

It was nearly ten when he woke up the next morning, his mouth dry and his stomach feeling heavy as lead. He got up and poured some cold water from the jug into a basin. Outside he could see a street of warehouses lined with vans and drays being loaded up. The sun was shining from over behind the hotel and there was steam coming up off the pavements, still wet from the last night's rain. He washed his face with cold water and rinsed out his mouth. The water in the carafe smelled bad so he drank from the bedroom jug instead. He rang a bell that hung down beside the bed. After a while, when nothing had happened, he rang again. A girl put her head round the door.

"What is it?" she said.

"I want some tea."

"It's too late for tea. It's after ten."

"I suppose it's too late for breakfast?"

"We don't serve after half-past nine." She looked at him disfavourably.[2]

"All right," Johnson said. "I don't want anything."

She closed the door, going out. Johnson lay back in bed, then a thought struck him and he sat up and looked in his pockets. His money was still there and he lay back again.

He was trying to make up his mind what to do, running his eye over the pink-flowered wallpaper and the faded yellow

2   disfavourably] *original read* disfavouredly

curtains and the white-plastered roof. I'll get out of this town, he said, that's one thing I'll do.

When he was dressed and shaved, a little later, he went down into the lounge and through and into the bar. They were putting out counter lunch along the bar. He drank half a glass of beer and ate some bread and cheese sandwiches and felt better. When he went back into the lounge he saw the man called Tom that he had heard talking the night before. He looked as strong and red-faced in the daylight as he had at night and wore the same riding-leggings and check coat and shirt. Johnson went up to him and asked him:

"I'm looking for work on a farm. Have you got any jobs?"

The big man looked him up and down. He looked Johnson over in a way that was aggressive, but not offensive. He said:

"Cadet?"

Johnson shook his head, not understanding him.

"I mean do you want to learn farming or d'you want a job?"

"I want a job."

"Can you milk?"

"I was brought up on a farm. It's a while since I was on one. I expect I can milk."

The big man looked at him in silence for a moment.

"I get a lot of fellows asking for jobs," he said. "Not all of them want them. You're just out?"

"I got here yesterday."

"In the war?"

Johnson nodded.

"I reckon we ought to help fellows that were in the war," the big man said heavily. "I'll tell you what. Name's Blakeway. I'll give you my address. Farm's fifty miles south of here, dairy farm, one hundred and twenty cows. You turn up there two to three days from now when I'm back. I'll know then if you want the job. Most of you fellows that come out here'd rather stay in town. Good men are scarce. I'll give you a chance at it."

He scribbled his name and address on a piece of paper. He nodded then and went off. Johnson asked the hotel-keeper later that day about him.

"He's got money," the hotel-keeper said. "He's got money all right, but he's mean as death. He'll die of blood pressure one of these days."

CHAPTER II

Going down to the farm by service car was seeing a new country open out like the raw edges of a wound. It had a green, rich, unfinished look. The road ran out into loose metal and ruts through low hills half-cleared, and farm-houses, wooden, unpainted. Where the land was cleared as it was for miles at a time with fences and no hedges, the grass grew springing with life.

"Top-dressing," said Sam, the little Maori car-driver, smoking green Three Castle and driving with one hand. "They spread it like butter hereabouts."

Johnson got to the farm in the slack period after lunch. It was a large farm with a great iron milking-shed as big as a village hall, the farm-house half a mile in from the road surrounded by dark pines. The dairy flats ran in from the banks of the dark Waikato. They stretched for miles with only cows and odd sheds and pine trees to break them, as flat and dull as the back of your hand. He walked up to the farm-house from the road, his suit-case in his hand, feeling dusty and awkward in city clothes.

No one came to the front door when he knocked, so he went out again and through the yard to the back door. He knocked there twice and a woman called to come in. It was dark in the kitchen coming in from the light and warmth with the stove burning and the smell of food. A pale, middle-aged woman sat at the table and there was an old lady in a rocking-chair by the fire. She was very old. She wore a long black dress and a white lace cap, and looked like Queen Victoria grown thin and asleep. Johnson explained himself shortly. The woman at the table smiled palely.

"Tom rang up about you," she said. "Sit down. Have some tea. The men'll be in soon." She poured some tea and cut bread and butter. The old woman by the fire woke up suddenly.

"Who's that?" she said sharply. "Who's there?"

Blakeway's wife leaned over and touched her arm.

"It's all right, Mother," she said; the old woman leaned back in sleep again. Johnson answered questions about himself, talking quietly.

Milking at the Blakeways' was as much like working in a factory as anything else. It passed the first day as it did in all the three years he was there, in steam and the warm smell of milk and cows and the noise of the motor-engine that worked the machines. They showed him how to strip the cows and wash them and drive them out when they were milked dry. There were one hundred and twenty cows and five men[3] working for three hours evening and morning to milk them.

Afterwards he went over to a little hut against the farm-house where he was to live, and washed and changed his shirt. He talked there for a time before they went into the house to eat, with a man, Scott, who was to share this hut with him. These men he talked to did not worry him very much. They were not curious about him. Finding he came from England, they were not interested to inquire further. They let it go at that, being interested in the things in front of them.

This Scott was a small man and dark, with a moustache like a Mexican, and kind and tired-looking eyes. He stood with hands in his belt below his hips, in the doorway, looking out at the night coming down over the pine trees.

"I wasn't in the war," he told Johnson. "No, boy, no war for me. M'chest's bad so they said. It's a good thing it's over now."

3   five men] men

And Johnson, sitting on the doorstep, was trying to roll a cigarette.

"You got to pack it fairly tight," Scott said, "and roll it round a bit. You want to pull the end off and shake it down. They're better than anything you'll buy."

"He's not a bad old sod," he said, a little later of Blakeway, "only it's an easier life when he's off the farm. The missis is all right. Her scones is good. They had a daughter used to be here, Eileen, that was all right, only she's gone off now into town. You can't blame them with wages being the way they are and work the way it is in the country. The old girl in there is crazy as a coot."

It was not long before Johnson was at home in this country. He talked as they all talked. He got to know the dates of the race meetings and where to get beer in town at most times, and the story of the 1905 match when Wales beat the All Blacks by one try to nil, and why it was necessary to have a farmers' government to protect the real interests of the country.

Going in to Hamilton on Saturday nights after milking with Scotty and the others on the farm Ford lorry, and perhaps dancing or just drinking and talking in the back of the 'Central', was as good a time as he could want then. Coming home late at night and perhaps singing 'Abe' and 'Swanee' over the dark roads where the man who drove had still to be thinking, or warm and asleep in the back of the van, and coming in quietly to the farm-house so that the dogs would know them and not bark. Blakeway cut his wages when the first slump came in 1921, but raised them again in 1922, and all the time the warm rain came down and the grass grew thick and green and the cows came into the milking-shed heavy with cream.

"It's only the old bull has a good time on this farm," said Scotty, and Johnson grinned, hosing down the concrete floor after milking time.

They used to talk at times, Johnson and Scott, about buying a farm. Everybody wanted to buy a farm sooner or later in New Zealand. You didn't buy a farm and build a house and grow pine trees round it to stay there, but to sell it to somebody else and live on the profit. To hear two farmers talk the towns were full of men who had sold farms for the profit and an easy life. Blakeway and his missis had lived there twenty years. They were always trying to sell their farm. Blakeway had missed the best times just after the war; he felt badly about this. Now there mightn't be any good times again, not really good times, no half a crown a pound times, not in their time.

Scott had the ideas about buying a farm, getting in on a small deposit, on a soldier settlement, working share-milking to make the money first, and Johnson listened desultorily, having no ambition. Johnson went to dances with Mabel from the small farm two miles down the road. He walked out with her and kissed her in the back of a car[4] at dances, Mabel at twenty-three, strong, solid, and wanting a husband.

Mabel's father had ideas about buying a farm.

"You don't want to go on taking wages from that red-faced bastard all your life," he said. "You want to keep your eye out for a bit of land."

"I'd work ten years before I bought an acre round here," Johnson said.

"You get a good team of horses and hire them out and work around with them. You make money that way. You want to get half-cleared land and bush land and clear it. That's what you want to do. The missis and I chopped firewood outside the back door when we moved in here."

4   a car] the car

His face was grizzled over a drooping grey moustache, but the lines of his face were well formed and well fed. His wife, Mabel's mother, was a short plump woman with arms as powerful as a horse's leg, but her feet were troubling her.

"There's only one thing you want to be a farmer," Mabel's father said, "that's a good partner, that's one like my old woman. Someone'll work with you, cook with you, not one of these going off into town running up doctor's bills. That's the first thing a man wants."

"He wants a bit of land," Johnson said. "He wants a little capital."

Mabel's father was back in the old days, the pioneer days, when you had to bake bread if you wanted to eat bread, no groceries coming in three times a week on the cream-lorry. Mabel's grandfather had shot Maoris for his bit of land. Mabel had ideas about farms, but they ran on Scotty's lines with a small deposit and a government scheme;[5] and Johnson listened desultorily, having no ambition.

Scotty talked to him persuasively.

"You and I could make a nice job of a little farm," he said, "up back there Pirongia way.[6] First we'd have just the few cows, keep us going like. Then when we'd cleared a bit we'd run sheep. Then more sheep. After a time, no bloody cows, just condensed milk and sheep and good holidays in winter before lambing time. Come ten years you could sell out on that."

"You'd want money to start up like that," Johnson said.

"You don't want so much."

"Maybe I'll marry Mabel, get her old man's farm."

"You won't get that farm except on a mortgage that'll sweat your guts out. That old man isn't giving nothing away."

5   a government scheme] the government scheme
6   back there Pirongia way] back there in the hills

"I'm not so sure."

"I'm bleeding well sure."

Mabel didn't like Scotty.

In Huntly with the miners they were drinking one night; it was an old soldiers' night. Scotty got to talking with one man, a tall, gaunt riding-man. He called Johnson over.

"Listen, Johnnie," he said, "this fellow's got a farm he wants working. This is my mate, Johnson," he said. "We work together." Scotty having drunk a lot quickly wouldn't let either of them talk.

"This is the thing, Johnnie," he said. "Here's Thompson here got the farm I was telling you of, Pirongia way.[7] One man can't work it. Three men could work it like nobody's business."

The tall man nodded, not smiling, and Johnson having drunk all he needed to drink that night, nodded too.

"We could work that farm like nobody's business," said Scotty warmly, his hat pulled down over his forehead, squinting with one eye.

"We ought to have a look at this farm," Johnson said, contributing something to the conversation.

"We'll come right up and have a look at it, next week-end."

"How'll we get there?"

"We'll borrow the truck and drive up."

"You can't drive up, not in winter," the tall man said. "You'll have to ride in. It's thirty miles from here."

The stewards were going round filling glasses from enamel jugs.

"We'll drink to your farm," Scotty said when their glasses were filled.

"Yes, sir, the farm," Johnson said, feeling heavy and solid.

7   telling you of, Pirongia way] telling you of

The thin man who owned it said nothing.

Two weeks after that they packed up and moved in to the farm, hiring two riding horses and a pack-horse for the ride, giving Blakeway one week's notice and getting cursed for it. Johnson didn't mind the change very much. He was young then. The country was still new to him and he believed what Scotty said. Mabel didn't mind much. There were other young men in the district. Johnson had the idea at first that after a while he might marry Mabel and she could move up and cook for them, but he changed his mind after he had got to the farm. There was only a small hut for the three of them to live in with bunks around it and a lean-to kitchen, and it was fairly clear that short of another world war there wouldn't ever be money to build a house. So he forgot about Mabel.

Chapter III

When they left Blakeway's that Saturday, they took their packs into Huntly and hired horses there. It was too late to start out that night so they slept at a little hotel and got off early in the morning. When they had ridden all morning, they began to climb out of the Waikato Valley and the dairy country into the fern foot-hills of Pirongia.[8] The sun was hot and the clay road winding up the ridges was dusty.

"They paid the bastards by the chain to make these roads," Scotty said. It was an old joke.

Leaving the green Waikato behind them was like going out of a land of plenty into desert. On the scrub hills there was little grass and no life. In half-cleared patches, sometimes they saw starved ewes or cattle running wild. There were few farms[9] and they met no one on the road.

In the afternoon they stopped where the road came out on a ridge to rest the horses. From there they could see across the plains to Huntly and Hamilton[10] and the river bending away eastward where it turned into the pumice country. It was a clear day with a heat haze on the hills and southward, a hundred miles away, the hot sun shimmered on the snow peaks of Ruapehu. Johnson had never seen a snow mountain before. It looked dwarfed and toy-like at that distance, rising out of the heart of the bush country.

"It's a bloody marvellous country," he said. "By God, Scotty, I wouldn't mind climbing that mountain there."

Scotty, pushing his hat forward over his eyes, rolling a

8   the fern foot-hills of Pirongia] the fern hills
9   few farms] a few farms
10   Huntly and Hamilton] Hamilton

cigarette, grunted.

"That's a daft idea," he said. "I'm thinking right now we're bloody fools to be up in these bone-dry blasted hills. There's——all grows up here."

The hills grew more lonely as the afternoon went on, until Johnson came to dislike them. As the sun set they could see lights coming out on the plains thirty miles below, but around them were only odd pin-points of farm-houses hidden away from the road they were following. Scotty was silent and Johnson depressed, leading his tired pack horse. It was nearly midnight before they came to the farm. Thompson was asleep, but got up and kicked the fire together and made them tea which they drank, eating tinned beef and bread.

"I thought you'd turned it in," Thompson said. It was hard to tell whether he was pleased to see them or not. He put the horses out into the home paddock and made them up beds on the floor, for there was only one bunk in the hut. Johnson slept, tired out, with Scotty rolled up in blankets on the floor, his head on a saddle. When the fire died down in the early morning it grew very cold, almost as if there were[11] a frost outside, but he turned over and went to sleep again, to be woken at six by Thompson stumbling over them to get the fire going again. It was Sunday morning. He had already been out to get the cows in and now came back to the house to make tea and to get one of them to help him milk.

That day Scotty rode back with the horses, stayed the night in town, and came back the next day riding part way on a cream-lorry and walking the rest. Johnson and Thompson worked round the hut, putting up new bunks and clearing room for three of them to live. It meant putting all the harness

11 were] was

and tools which had filled up the living-room outside and building a lean-to to cover them.

The new farm lay up among the fern-hills. It looked north and westward over bush roads to the coast, and from the ridges down on to the golden butter plains. On this new farm there were ten cows and very little grass, one working horse and a Maori hack and a few pigs. Thompson bought two hundred sheep that autumn with his last money when they moved in and fifty of them died of cold and starvation in the winter. They milked the cows by hand and if there was any cash from sales it went back into the farm, which was covered with fern and blackberry, and looked ready to swallow any amount of money.

They made an agreement in writing when they moved in about the profits and ownership of the farm, but there weren't any profits. The cream money went on stores and tobacco and grass seed and fencing wire. It was fairly clear that Thompson still owned the farm. He looked at Johnson and at Scott, and Johnson could see that he knew them as two men who would get tired of it and take their packs and move on. So he looked at them and decided he would get what work out of them he could.

Thompson got up first each morning at five and earlier in summer. He kicked the fire together; it never went out. Then he would make tea and Johnson would get up and pull on his boots and go out and milk with him. Scotty never got up before six; it was a covenant he had made with himself. Scotty got breakfast, porridge and bacon, and oatmeal scones when he felt good, and when the other two came back they would all eat and go off for the day. One or two days a week Scotty would stay behind and get wood and do whatever needed doing round the place. He had more domestic feeling than the others and liked to keep the hut clean.

It wasn't long before they began to quarrel.

"This is a co-operative outfit, this farm, not a Russian bloody slave camp," Scotty said.

Thompson was scornful.

"I'm still bossing it," he said.

"You're bossing it, yes, you're bossing it all right, but we work when we want to, see?"

"You're just a bloody little runt. You won't work mornings. You won't work Sundays. Listen, that Saturday night I met you and our homey here, d'you know that was the first day off I'd had in a year and a half? You wouldn't know what working is."

"He isn't human, Johnnie," Scott said afterwards. "He just isn't human."

Thompson had a cattle dog he liked. It was the only thing on the farm he liked. It was an old black and tan, scarred and beaten, and only good for getting cows in. Thompson brought it into the hut at nights and Scott would kick it out until Thompson swore at him and then the dog stayed scratching itself, flea-bitten, by the fire.

Thompson and Johnson talked at nights about the war. Thompson had an obsession about the war. He was going over it in his mind again, remembering every piece of it, the battles and the men and the names of places and talking about it till Scott shouted:

"Christ, turn it in. I wasn't at the war," and Thompson said nothing, looking at him, pale, gaunt, contemptuous.

"No," he said, after a time, "you wasn't in the war."

There were a lot of memories of the war in that part of the world. The valley was haunted by strange men who had been to the war. There was a man called Drake, two miles down the clay road, with one arm, who walked round all day shooting rabbits and couldn't farm; and another man whose axe slipped into his leg below the knee one day when he was out at the back, splitting fence posts. He bled to death, and lay for a week before anyone thought of looking for him, and when they found him the blood was black and dry where he had crawled half-way up the track to home, and there were flies on him. You seldom met your neighbours in this valley except when they had trouble, and came together to help one another, and then there was no time to talk. No one else talked about the war except Thompson. They had, most of them, been to the same places and done the same things, but they didn't want to talk about them and, with only Johnson to talk to, Thompson gave it up and talked to himself.

Johnson stood a year and a half and then with the summer coming in again decided to move on. He was going, as far as Thompson and the farm were concerned, without sympathy or regret, but was sorry to leave Scotty, with the lank hair and the twisted drooping moustache, the man who had shown him how to roll his cigarettes. He told him so. Scotty was not leaving.

"All my life I[12] been walking on," he told Johnson. "Maybe things will pick up here, we're getting more in grass each year."

"You'll go crazy, you and Thompson. He's a hell of a man."

"He'll be better, just the two of us, he'll be glad I'm here then, with the milking and all."

"He won't ever be glad of anything, that man."

So Johnson left. He went off early one morning with his pack, leaving a lot of clothes he didn't want. Thompson had gone off and neither had said good-bye, but Scotty came down the track to the bend of the clay road and patted him on the shoulder, liking him as he said good-bye.

12 I] I've

Chapter IV

He still had a little money in the savings bank at Huntly that hadn't gone into Thompson's farm, and he drew this out and moved north lazily, travelling the road.

He meant to stay in Auckland and see city life, but when he got there he couldn't like it. It was too noisy after the country, and the summer was coming in and the air smelt good from the hills west of the city and the sunlight splendid on the blue Coromandel range across the gulf. He moved on north through the fern-hills and the clay to the gum-fields beyond Whangarei. It was warm and he slept out at night.

There wasn't anything to do in the gum-fields. The *kauri* gum was all worked out and the gum-diggers had gone or lived on Maori farms and old-age pensions, so Johnson came in one day to a little hotel on a long tidal arm of the sea, lying up among pine trees and looking down on mangroves and the warm smell of mud. He put his swag down on the veranda and the proprietor, coming out from lunch, brought him a bottle of beer from the room inside that served as a bar.

"You don't get a drink anywhere else within twenty miles of here," he said. He was a red-haired man with mean blue eyes. The beer was warm but tasted good.

There was an old gentleman sitting on a rocking-chair on the veranda, an old fellow in a white coat, a man of about sixty with white hair and a white moustache and very red face.

He woke up to talk to Johnson when the owner had gone inside again. He asked him a lot of questions about himself.

"It's a nice place here," he said. "I'm thinking of settling here. It's nice and quiet and plenty of sun."

"It'd be just too quiet for me,' Johnson said.

'It's all right and very restful,' the old man said, nodding his fat red face. "When you've seen all the world I have and forty years in the Indian Army, my boy, you won't ask more than this. You play cards at all?"

"A little."

"Poker, eh?"

"I play it a little."

"You stay on here to-night and we might make up a little game," the old man said, and, folding his hands across his stomach, he dozed off to sleep.

Johnson helped the red-haired pub-owner to make a fence along the bottom of his garden through the afternoon. In the evening after they had all had a meal, Johnson and the old man sat out on the veranda with a pack of cards. The red-haired pub-owner watched them for a while, not liking it. It was nice sitting there on the veranda. The tide was coming in over the mud-reaches pushing a line of foam with it and the mud-holes cracking open as it came. The air was soft and warm with a scent of pine and fern and warm mangrove mud. Only the moths and mosquitoes drawn to the lamp were a nuisance. The old man, who was called Captain Dawson, ordered some whisky and gave Johnson a cigar to keep the mosquitoes away.

The old man was not very interested in varieties of card games. He liked playing show-poker, just turning up the cards to see which way they fell. He lost to Johnson a bit at first and raised the stakes. After they had played for an hour and a half he owed Johnson three pounds and went into his room to get some money.

The pub-owner kept coming in and out and watching them. While the old man was away he bent over the table and said to Johnson:

"Listen, don't take any more of his money."

"Why not," Johnson said. "It's quite good money, ain't it?"

"He don't know what he's doing. He shouldn't be playing cards at all."

"He knows what he's doing as well as I do. He's just unlucky."

"Listen, you bastard," the pub-owner said, "I'm supposed to look after the Captain. He's not supposed to play cards."

"Well, you tell him," Johnson said, but when the old man came back at that point the pub-owner said nothing except to grunt:

"It's getting late, Cap," but the old man took no notice, breathing heavily as he sat down. He raised the stakes again and it wasn't long before he owed Johnson five pounds. After that he started cutting aces high at a pound a time to get some of it back. Johnson lost twice, then won four times in a row, he lost once again, then won three times running. The hotel-keeper was standing beside him sweating. He couldn't stand the sight of the pound notes on the table. But the old man didn't seem to mind.

"You've cleaned me out, son," he said, and shook hands with Johnson, dividing the last of the whisky with him. After a while he went off to bed.

The pub-keeper turned on Johnson.

"You hand that over to me, you bastard," he said. "That's three weeks' board and lodging you got there and I seen the way you handled those cards."

"You tell it to the Captain," Johnson said. He had drunk some whisky and felt warm and very pleased with himself.

"Listen, you know why the Captain comes and lives down here? It's because he can't keep off the races and gamblin' in town. So he lives down here and I pretend I don't play, see? I promised his family. And then you come down here and throw those cards around the way I seen you."

"He might just as well've won," Johnson said. "It's the way the cards were falling. I don't often get a run like that."

"You hand that nine pounds back to me."

"Or what?" said Johnson, and got up.

He locked the door of his room and would have shut the window only it was too hot, but he backed a chair against it and tied the mosquito curtains across to make it difficult for anyone to get in quietly. He was still laughing as he went to sleep and when he went off in the morning he had to laugh again. The Captain wasn't about when he took the road and the red-haired man said nothing as he paid his bill.

A week later he got a job working on a coastal scow. He was sitting on the end of a wharf one day watching the tide come up the river and three Maori children fishing with tea-tree rods from the end of the wharf, and waiting for one of them to fall in. He was sitting there because it was dry and pleasant sitting in the sun before it got too hot with the heat of the day. The river was narrow and deserted, with tea-tree hills coming down to it on both sides, and no houses in sight. A clay track led away from the wharf and disappeared into the hills. Beyond that there was nothing and nobody in sight. While he sat there, the scow came round the bend of[13] the river with its grey sails slack in the wind and its auxiliary engine chugging softly. It was a large, flat-bottomed boat with a white streak round the water-line and a blunt bow. It tied up alongside the wharf and Johnson watched while the captain and his Maori deck-hand put two large packing cases ashore. The captain was a fair-haired, grizzled giant of a man with a drooping moustache. He said to Johnson:

"The lazy b——s here won't build a shed. If this stuff lies

13 of] in

here a week and gets wet, it won't be me to blame." He turned to the oldest of the Maori boys.

"Say, you," he said. "You run off and tell Jack his stuff's here." The boy grinned. He shuffled his feet and rolled his eyes so that the whites showed, looking at the other two boys. They all giggled, but did not move. The captain gave it up.

"There's no sense anywhere in this part of the country," he said. He sat down heavily on the end of the wharf and talked to Johnson while he filled his pipe. After a while, he offered to take Johnson down with him to the whale-fishing town of Whangamumu.

"You want to smell that place just once," he said. "Though it's not as good as it used to be. The whales don't come down the coast any more."

He was in no hurry and waited for the tide to turn. In the early afternoon they cast off and backed the scow laboriously round and went downstream. The Maori children were still on the wharf. After Whangamumu, Petersen, the captain and owner, offered Johnson a job as an extra hand for a pound a week and his keep. He was not very useful on the ship, but Petersen and the half-caste Maori cook did the sailing and Johnson helped with the heavy work of loading when they had a load and learned to run the engine.

Those were good times for him. They covered all the small bays of the north, going up the winding rivers to drop stores at deserted wharf-heads, coming down with wool or cattle, or sometimes long rafts of logs for Whangarei, when the drag behind would hold them until they were hardly moving on the open sea. There were days adrift and in no hurry, going up the coast, waiting for the sea-breeze to come in, the great boom creaking across, and a hot sun beating down on them. And there were days, too, waiting in Tutukaka for the gale to blow over, two anchors out, and the sharp gusts shivering as they came across the hill, the white thunder of surf outside, and ashore, warm fires and company.

They were good days along the coast. 'Moonlight and Roses' and 'Show me the Way to go Home' were the songs they sang then, and the Maori girls singing and an accordion playing outside the little dance halls as they came in of an evening, the air warm, and young men from the cruising yachts laughing as they rowed ashore. Tom Blake, the Maori cook, would have disappeared ashore and Johnson and Petersen would be sitting there, the deck just lifting to the swell from outside the bay. They would sit there and smoke and talk, though not much, and watch the moon coming up in the sky and the lights ashore, and the riding lights of the yachts and their own light on the mast-head shaking slowly across the sky.

Petersen had travelled. He was a Swede, born in Nova Scotia. He had worked on a whaler and round the islands. He had been married twice, once in San Francisco and once in Singapore: the first wife had died and the second had disappeared. He was sixty years old. He talked about men he had met and places he had seen sometimes, but not very often. He was a simple man. He cared a lot for the old *Sea-Spray*, which was his life[14] savings. He tried to explain to Johnson the ambitions of personal ownership, but Johnson said:

"This country's all right for me as it is. I don't worry about not having a ship of my own, Pete. I don't worry about that any more than I worried about not having a farm. There isn't any better country than this, not where a man can go about and get work, and stop when he wants to, and make money when he needs it, and take a holiday when he feels ready for one."

14 life] life's

Petersen grunted. He said:

"You're bloody young still and that's the way it was with me and it's the way all sailors live, but the last ten years I started saving. You got to start saving and looking after yourself some time. If I'd started earlier, I'd be better off. Listen, I went about thirty years. That time, if there was profits on the voyage, who got it? I didn't."

"If there was a loss you got wages."

"Sometimes, I didn't. Profit on the voyage and you got your wages and nothing else, no profit and you got what you damned well could. You know why fellows[15] go on living like that? Because it's easy. It's easy to take what's going and move on somewhere else."

"I don't mind," Johnson said. "It suits me."

"It suits you now all right. It won't always suit you. If I didn't think you were all right I wouldn't think you were such a bloody fool."

Johnson had changed by then. He was stronger than he had ever been before, his skin bronzed and roughened, and his hair bleached white. He was alive with the sun and the sleepiness of salt air and the long days at sea. He didn't worry about anything Petersen said. He was in charge of himself and he did not worry.

It was easy not to worry working for Petersen, he was the philosophic type. There were bonuses at Christmas, or when things were going well, and when things were going badly he swore to himself and never to anyone else. When there was an election in 1928 no one of them voted. Tom Blake couldn't write and didn't know where his home was, Petersen couldn't remember ever having voted, and Johnson didn't believe he

15 fellows] the fellows

was a resident. When the Liberals got in Tom Blake said the
Labour men were sore because their programme had been
stolen. Petersen roared with laughter reading the pink-covered
weekly that sometimes came aboard.

"Borrow seventy millions," he said. "Borrow, boom, and
bust."

"Seventy millions," Johnson said, "that's a lot of money."

"By God, it's a lot of money," Petersen said. "It's fifty pounds
each, by God. Yes, sir, we'll all get our piece of that. Fifty
pounds, I'll get those sails patched so you won't know 'em."

"Me," said Tom Blake. "I'm buying a little sailing boat with
mine, yes, Cap, just a small boat with maybe a little motor and
stay around doing fishing."

"Let's hope they get it quick," Petersen said. "I don't believe
there's that much money loose around the world."

But the good life came to an end in 1930. By then the
railway was through to the north; roads were being opened up
and the river trade was almost gone. The little that was left of it
was taken from them by a new diesel-engined and sail-less ship
that covered their ground in half the time and always on time,
with the roar of her engine shaking the cliffs. Tom Blake got
off at Whangaruru to settle down and grow melons and brew
bad drink from tree-bark. Petersen and Johnson took the ship
down to Auckland to be sold for breaking up. They made their
last trip against a cold south-westerly wind and were glad when
they had brought her in. Johnson sculled the dinghy ashore
and came back with food and a bottle of whisky. They cooked
steak over the oil stove in the cabin and sat afterwards drinking
whisky through the evening. Petersen's grizzled eyebrows and
blue eyes sunk deep beneath them had not changed in any
of the time Johnson knew him. He sat now not talking and
smoked his pipe, spitting all the time on the floor of the cabin.

They went to bed late and the next morning Johnson took his things and went ashore. It was going to be some time before the deal for the ship went through and there was nothing for him to do on board.

CHAPTER V

That was the last of the good years, though Johnson didn't know it at the time—1930, when everyone had money and the war was long over and never coming again. What's a Wall Street crash down there in the South Pacific, or reparations with the summer coming in and the price of butter fat still good? Nineteen-thirty—the second year of the talkies and 'Gold Diggers of Broadway', Al Jolson and 'Sonny Boy' already a memory. In the town, picture theatres were going up and new hotels and always full. Johnson moved down the Waikato, looking for Scotty. He wanted company. Thompson had gone, they told him at Huntly, and no one knew of Scotty, and then, at the 'Central' in Hamilton, he got news of him. He was working, cow-punching, they said satirically, at the Government farm, so he got word to him and Scotty came into town.

Scotty had grown older, there were streaks of white along the sides of his hair. He smoked more and coughed more and his eyelids drooped a little, but he still wore his slouch hat and moustache like a Mexican. He was shame-faced explaining himself.

"Just the rouse-about," he told Johnson. "Just the old farm-hand, milking and clearing up after the boys that are learning to farm. Me that was working up to own a farm—it's the hell, ain't it?"

"And Thompson?"

"You know, Johnnie," he said. "I even feel sorry for that bastard, that's the way I am. He was a mean man, he was mean as dirt. We'd go for months there not talking and me tearing my guts out clearing his logs. But they got him in the

55

end, yes, sir, they sold him up. That farm wasn't no good. It'd break any man, it was poor country. Everybody knew it was poor country. Only Thompson wouldn't ever admit that, not Thompson, so in the end the company had to tell him. Where's Thompson? I dunno. Gone off somewhere."

Scotty didn't need any persuading to start travelling again, though he looked mournful gazing down at his beer when Johnson suggested it.

"I guess that's the thing to do," he said. "There's wages on the railroads makes my mouth water, twelve and six a day and no questions, no piece-work, no trouble."

"We could do that," Johnson said, "clean up and have a bit in hand for the winter."

"I reckon so. I guess I will," Scotty said, still mournful. "I've kept clear of that pick and shovel work all my life. I'm a farming man, but I reckon I will."

So they went south together through the King Country and farther. They crossed over to the South Island, picked fruit and hoed tobacco through the summer, then went on the railway again in from Nelson and lived easy on public works. By autumn they were coming back again through the Wairarapa.

Prices began to fall in 1931. Wool went first, it had been going down for two years, and butter followed it. There was talk in the pubs at that time of slump and depression and currency reform. Someone got hold of Scotty on the sheep farm, where they had two weeks' work, and loaded him up with it so that he could talk of nothing else.

"Ye see, Johnnie," he said. "It's this way. There's so much in the country like what you and I might be making, lamb and wool and the like. Then there's so much money, not real money, mind you, but bank-notes, just printed off. Well, it doesn't suit these boys to print enough."

"Why doesn't it?"

"Well, see, they've got most of them as it is. If there's only a little of this money it's worth more, see?"

"Yes, I see that."

"Well, naturally then, that's how it is. There ain't enough money, see, so prices fall and who gets the hell of that? Why, you and me do."

"Well, so what? So what are you and me going to do?"

"I'll tell you. All it needs is the right men in charge and we could clear this up in a week. Listen, I'll tell you something. The way things are now, d'you know what's going to happen?"

"No, d'you?"

"I'll tell you. There'll be a real farmers' party that'll clear this up. The fellows they get in now, they're just yes-men. They do what they're told. D'you think these fellows are going to stand for that with prices falling the way they are? Not much, they're not. No, Johnnie, a real farmers' Government that'd take hold and run these banks, that's what's going to happen."

"Sounds all right," Johnson said.

"You bet it sounds all right."

They were in a small Wairarapa town after that job ended in time for a 'Cheer-up Week'. The organizers hadn't got Scotty's idea. They had another idea, that all you had to do was to start spending again and get the money moving around so quickly that it couldn't ever rest. The main street was decorated with fern-leaves and electric lights. There were processions and prizes and a fair amount of small change spent on bunting and coloured paper. Scotty and Johnson watched the procession.

There was a crowd of young men in it dressed up as cowboys on horses and one as Queen Boadicea in a milk-cart. There was a brass band and they were singing. They were singing the American song then, 'Happy Days are Here Again'. They were singing very loudly and happily, some of them with drink and mostly with the excitement of being in a crowd together with the band playing. They were conducting a ceremony. They were burying an effigy called 'General Depression' in the public lavatory in the centre of the town. This was shocking some of the older city councillors a little, but most of the crowd seemed to like it all right.

This 'cheer-up' movement suited Johnson. He had usually spent the money he earned as he got it.

"I must be a good citizen," he said. He was saying this to an old man beside him over a drink afterwards, for business in the bars was still good. This old man had white hair and a long nose with a thin, rather mean, face. He said:

"Son, I seen a depression before when I was a boy and it wasn't so good. It'll take more than those young sods out there to bury this one."

The man behind the bar laughed.

"Roll on good times," he said.

By the end of that year the bottom was falling out of everything, falling so far that it never seemed likely to come back again.

Johnson felt the temper of the country changing. It had always been a lucky country, a country where, if a man were well and strong, he could wander about and live well and eat well, where everybody was your friend in a hard, casual way, where a man tramping the roads in the back country could be sure of a night's rest and a meal wherever he stopped. It was strange to see how things changed now that the luck had turned, how people grew uneasy and careful with each other, and kept to themselves, watching and saving what they had.

Johnson and Scotty worked through the winter on a railway in west of the King Country. It was wet, cold, miserable work, but there was still pay to be had. Scotty's cough grew worse with living and working in the damp, sticky clay so that he had to take days off. No one believed the line would ever be finished. It was being made in patches, a cutting here and an embankment there. They had given up laying sleepers and rails, and concentrated on digging which needed no equipment and little skill.

When the spring came, and the farming season got under way again, they went north. They were looking for work in the dairy country where Johnson had begun twelve years before. They wanted to try share-milking; they had ideas of living and farming by themselves, but there were no jobs of that kind going. Farmers were doing their own milking, talking of mortgages and waiting for the stock companies to foreclose. They went back to Blakeway's and found that the farm had changed hands four years before. They called on Mabel's father and found him still alive and still working. He told Johnson he was no good:

"The country's rotten with fellows like you," he said.

Mabel was married and had two children. Her husband had a post-office store on the Auckland road. She made tea for Johnson and Scotty when they called.

"It's no life for women on the land," she said. "You don't get a minute to yourself."

"You're well out of that, Johnnie," Scotty said afterwards, while they waited by the road to pick up a lift. "She's a mean woman, you can tell it by the way she watches her husband while he eats."

Things were bad in Auckland. The first thing they knew they were out of money and standing in a food queue.

"There's no sense in this," Scotty said. "These towns never did me any good."

"It's a hell of a way to live," Johnson said. "I've got a feeling it's always this way in town."

He wanted to go on north and get into the country again, but Scotty wouldn't go.

"You've seen the way the country is, Johnnie," he said. "We're better off here for the time being. Things can't go on this way. They can't keep all these fellows standing around here like this."

But the queues got longer with men coming in from the farms and they were very quiet. Fortunately the summer was on and the weather was warm, so that they slept out at night in the parks. Scotty found a place after that where they could doss down near a boat-building shed on the water-front. They got to know their way around the relief depots. Scotty, who was sick a good deal of the time, got several sets of clothes and boots, but Johnson still looked too well to be really effective in front of charity workers. Some of the days they spent walking round the suburbs asking for work from door to door and once or twice they got odd jobs in gardens. Scotty still read the papers each day in the library, but Johnson had given it up.

"Things can't go on this way," Scotty kept saying, but Johnson wasn't so sure. He felt badly about the way things were turning out.

"They're ruining my system," he said.

"What's your system?"

"It's the keep on working and moving, it's the hard work for the good time and never stay long anywhere."

"That's a hell of a system. That's what makes a fool of you. You know where you and I ought to be right now?"

"Not here."

"You're right, not here, you're bloody right. We oughta saved up and be on a bit of land we owned and just laying back careful-like till things blow over."

"A hell of a chance we had," and they stopped talking, but the conversation kept beginning again.

In January they were on relief work, tidying up the edges of roads, twenty men with pick-axes and shovels and spades moving down suburban roads with work to do that even the borough surveyor had difficulty in finding and a job to discover when it was done. Scotty got into an argument with a ratepayer going to work about the waste of money weeding the roads and was told by the foreman to shut his trap. In February, being unmarried men, they were sent out of town to a relief camp.

The work of the camp was making a scenic road that might, when there was ever money to metal or concrete it, be a tourist drive round[16] the city. It was slow work and monotonous, made slower because the work was done with picks and shovels instead of scoops. The work had to be made to last. In the long run it was the uselessness of the work which was wearying, rather than the work itself.

Johnson shared a tent with Scotty and two other men. Scotty had been finally diagnosed as consumptive and coughed miserably at nights. One of the others, Roach, a little Cockney not long out—'Pommy', they called him, and mimicked his speech—wanted him shifted, but the others did not mind. The fourth man was older, a grey-haired Scot named Robertson. His reserve and solidity appealed to Johnson; they worked together and shared clothes.

It was a passable routine when the weather was fine. When it rained and the cold came—and autumn seemed nearer to winter that year—life grew wretched and uncomfortable.

16 round] around

There was no floor to the tent and after a day's rain, mud and damp seemed to swallow everything. Even the one big meal-tent grew thick and squalid with men crowding into it to play cards or talk. There was nowhere to dry clothes when the men came in wet and heavy with clay from the roads. Johnson bore all this as the other men did because the camp and the work had a temporary and make-shift air about it. There was no money to put flooring down in the tents. If there had been money it would hardly have been worth while since the camp wasn't always going to be there. Things would 'pick up' soon and there would be real work and money in the country again.

The camp was in a dry area. Suburbs voted themselves dry periodically in Auckland and the camp lay inside one of these temperance areas, rather irrationally, for it was off the main roads and houses and in the thick of tea-tree hills. The nearest pub was down by the water-front, on an arm of the harbour, five miles away. The nearest picture-house was two miles away and only showed pictures three times a week.

Johnson was saving money. He had cut down on smoking. He didn't go into town if he could help it. He said to himself each morning as he got up, climbing into wet clay-heavy slacks, this is a hell of a thing, this comes of living in towns, I'll get to hell out of here the first thing I can, it can't be worse in the country. But men coming in every day to the camp from the country said it was worse, farmers were turning off old hands, working themselves the way they'd never worked before, getting sold up by the banks.

One Saturday, going over to the pub late in the afternoon because they couldn't stand it any longer, Johnson and Scotty had three drinks before closing time and bought two quart bottles each. They sat down off the road in the tea-tree, a mile out of camp on the way home, and drank them. After the walk and not having anything to eat and not having drunk for a long time, they got to feel good so that they were making plans again and Scotty was talking about farms and opportunities there were for men, now things were bad, to pick up something cheap. But it came on to rain with a light drizzle from the north as they were finishing the last of the beer, and walking back to camp Johnson was sick by the road. He remembered only getting into bed feeling bad and waking in the early morning with the light just coming in through the tent door and birds calling from the bush, dry-mouthed, listening to Scotty breathing heavily in his sleep and Robertson snoring, lying awake and saying to himself, I've got to get to hell out of this, this isn't any life for a man.

Johnson got to be unpopular because he wouldn't join the U.W.M., the Unemployed Workers Movement. He said to the organizer that asked him:

"I'm not a union man. I'm a farm worker."

"It doesn't give a damn what you used to be. You're unemployed now, ain't you?"

"All the same I never joined a union."

"You ought to. You got to stand together these days."

"And a hell of a lot you can stand together for. What you going to do? Go on strike? That's a good one."

Scotty told him afterwards:

"You ought to join. He's right, Johnnie, you got to get together."

"For what?"

"For better times. These are Labour men these fellows. I tell you[17] what's going to happen in this country, there's going to be a farmers' Government, see, with Labour, the fellows in the

17 I tell you] I will tell you

towns joining up with the fellows in the country and taking things out of the hands of the bankers and the politicians."

"Christ, they're all politicians," Johnson said.

But still most of the men went into the city for week-ends, crowding into open lorries on Saturday afternoons, the few married men to their families, the others for a night in town. And Johnson was getting unpopular, not joining the U.W.M., saving his money. He was saving about six shillings a week, taking off tobacco and a new pair of boots that he had had to buy when he started work. He had never been unpopular like that with a crowd of men before, but he kept saying to himself, to hell, they won't keep me here long.

He remembered one conversation that he had with Robertson not long before he left there. He was lying on his bunk in the deserted tent on a Saturday afternoon reading a magazine when Robertson came in and sat down, grunting stiffly as he unlaced his boots. He said:

"You're not in town with the boys?"

"Not to-day, Mac."

"They tell me it's beginning the football season," Robertson said.

"League maybe, I don't know. I never watched it."

Robertson lay back on his bunk folding his hands behind his head. The tent-door flapped open showing the line of tea-tree and a grey sky. The low hills around the camp were barren and desolate.

"Christ," he said, at length. Johnson was silent turning over a page. "Did ye never think of getting out of this country?" Robertson said.

"Not me," Johnson told him. "It's been all right for me."

Robertson raised himself fiercely on one elbow to look at him. "Ye don't think this is all right," he said.

"It'll be all right again."

"That's what the daft fellows here are all saying, the damn fools. You give them enough to eat—just enough—and a drink once a week, and they go on working day after day, working in muck for nothing. Is that all right? It'll get better. Who the hell knows it's going to get better?"

Johnson said, not laying down his book: "What's the use, Mac? You can't do anything. I'm getting out just as soon as I can."

Robertson lay down again.

"You can't do anything," he said more quietly. "No, you can't do anything. That's right. Or you won't do anything. I don't know. I'd give a lot to get home again, and mind, it's the first time I ever thought that." He had come out as a young man and worked all his life on a sheep farm in the South Island. It had taken a major depression to uproot him.

Johnson grinned at him. It was unusual to see him disturbed.

"Scotty's the one," Johnson said. "You ought to join up with him."

Robertson wrinkled his face disgustedly.

"That bloody social creditor," he said. "If he talked less, I'd listen more. The little bastard never worked anywhere till now. It's a har-rdship to him, by God."

"Scotty's all right," Johnson said. "He works all right. He's interested in politics, that's all."

Robertson was silent for a moment.

"I wouldn't clear out," Johnson said. "Not even if I could from this country. It's no better anywhere else. You've just to read the papers. Back in England now———"

"Ah, back in England, eh?"

"Sure, where's your working man's friend, Ramsay MacDonald now, eh?"

Robertson spat disgustedly over the side of his bunk.

"He wasn't ever a Scotsman," he said. "Everyone knew that. Did you never hear of Keir Hardie or Willie Gallacher?"

"Well, all you'd get'd be the dole, and you know it."

"It'd be a more gentlemanly life, boy. You're young—you wouldn't appreciate that. Just a few shillings the week[18] and a drink now and again and no useless bloody work to do. No rain, no mud, no digging holes for someone to fill them in again on a public works programme. None of that in the old country."

He breathed heavily, pulling the grey blanket up over his legs and relaxed, turning over on one side. When Johnson looked at him again he was asleep, breathing heavily, his mouth open beneath his grizzled grey moustache, the lines on his face old and tired. Johnson lay for a while not looking at his book, but at the stretched seam of the canvas over him. He was trying to think what he could do, how long he could stay there, and where he could go. To hell, he said, they won't keep me here, and he took up his book again.

18　the week] a week

CHAPTER VI

Going in on the lorry to the meeting, Johnson began to be sorry that he had promised to come. In the half-light after sunset the air was cold and as the lorry swayed round corners he hunched his coat up over his ears and tried not to listen to the Cockney, Roach, who talked endlessly, volubly. They had had an argument in the tent before they started, when Robertson refused to come. Sitting on the edge of his bunk he had watched them get ready.

"The demonstrator-rs," he said ironically, and Roach turned to him bustling and eager.

"You'd better come, Mac," he had said, his little eyes full of excitement, his voice squeaking indignantly. "This'll be the best thing we've done. They'll see they can't treat us like dirt, they will."

"That's what ye are," Robertson said, rolling a cigarette. He ran his eye over Roach with melancholy humour. "That's all ye are. Just dirt."

And Johnson had smiled, bending over the tent's one mirror to do his hair.

"You ought to come, Mac," he said, not turning round. "This is your chance to do something. You wanted something done."

"I never marched in a procession yet, man. I don't intend it now."

Roach spoke up again.

"We've got to hold together, mate," he said.

"That's right." It was Scotty. He wasn't feeling well. He stood thin and ill by the tent door, dressed in his only suit, ready to go.

"You oughtn't to go, Scotty," Johnson said. "You'd best turn in," but he grinned, shaking his head.

"I don't hold together," Robertson said. "I'm too old for that. And as for you, Roach, I'll be sleeping quietly here while they're breaking your head open."

"There'll be no head-breaking."

"Ay, there'll be head-br-reaking, all right. There's police in there waiting for every one of ye."

"It's a free country," Roach said. "We've a right to march in the streets."

"It's no sae free."

"We've a right to march in the streets to show the crying shame of what they've done to us, the way they're treating us."

Robertson finished rolling his cigarette and licked the gummed edge carefully.

"It's a fine, free country," he said. "Ye couldn't get a job so ye took relief. Now they cut your pay, so ye have a processi-on. Verra fine. Verra fine, na doubt. What d'ye think ye're getting, Roach man, walking the streets? Is it Douglas credit? Is it socialism? It is not. Ye'll get a thick head and no sleep and be back at work to-morrow two chains up the road with yer feet in the clay."

Johnson remembering this agreed with Robertson as they made the journey in. The men about him were half interested, looking for a night in town, a little excitement, a chance to walk the streets. They were angry about the way their wages had been cut, their 'starvation rates' of pay. They were angry, but they did not yet really care. The men who really cared were the married men and they for the most part had stayed in camp. Johnson himself had not stayed in camp, but he did not care.

They got off the lorry by the wharves west of the town and

formed up to march to the post office. The organisers from their camp had a banner, an old sheet, and daubed on it in black ink the slogan, 'West River Unemployed Camp. More pay. Real Work. No Slave Camps'. Two men marched at the head carrying this and Johnson fell in behind, keeping on the inside. The arrangement was that they should join with a procession of post and telegraph workers and march with them through the town to the town hall. No one from Johnson's camp had very clear ideas as to what would happen then. They fell into line and marched off along the water-front.

In the crowded space before the post office it became clear that the meeting and the procession had some meaning, at least in the numbers of people that it had drawn together. The streets were thick with people and the pavements lined. Trams had stopped running and there was no traffic going through. The head of the procession had already started on its way through the main street to the town hall. The West River contingent fought their way through the crowds to the centre of the square and joined the marchers, who were more than four abreast; they filled the street as they went forward. The West River standard disappeared to reappear again a few yards ahead of them. Johnson found himself with Roach and Scotty and some others, going slowly forward up the street.

In the grimness and tenseness of that mass of men a new spirit came over them. It was a very silent procession that marched, without bands or songs or shouting. Johnson going with them felt this change. He lost the sense of waste and frustration that had been with him. Instead he felt that he had a part in something. What it was he could not have said, but only that he was with men who shared his lack of fortune, who were the same as he was and had the same purpose; that they were going forward together, where, he could not say, but only that they were going somewhere and would be together. The same feeling had changed even Roach who marched beside him so that he no longer talked and joked and grumbled, but marched silently with his head up looking forward, and Scotty was no longer ill, but well-looking.

The onlookers who filled the pavements were silent, too, while they went by. At street corners, and here and there along the route, there seemed to be a great many policemen, occasionally mounted, their horses turning restlessly. When the marchers came to the open space by the town hall, the advance guard of post and telegraph workers had gone inside. The unemployed who followed them were being held up at the door. As more and more marching men pressed up behind them, the square became packed, and the silence that had been with them seemed to break ominously. There was a kind of murmured shouting and excitement that ran down the street and through the watching crowds as if they felt, not that anything was happening, but that something must. After the march, which had been a beginning, to be held in check like this made men angry: they shared between them an anger that was overwhelming.

Johnson fighting for a place in this press saw a mounted policeman on a great white horse trying to hold his ground at the head of the street. Not far from him, in the centre of the crowd where the street lamps were shining, he could see a man addressing the unemployed marchers, held up on their shoulders, his cap pulled up and waving in the air, the light shining on his sweating face. Johnson could see him, his mouth moving and his face working but could not hear what he said. The crowd moved round and round him like a broken tide-rip. Sometimes Johnson was carried in with it and at others thrown back again. There was no longer for him any moving where he wanted to go but only where everyone else was going, and there was still the feeling that it would be somewhere and that everyone would go.

The whole picture stayed like that for several minutes. Some men were still going into the hall, but the police were holding the unemployed back and the little man held up on their shoulders was still talking. Then two policemen went in towards him to try and stop him and there was a surge just as if the wave had spilled over and was rolling up the shore. Johnson saw a baton go up and an arm raised and the little man go down with a blow on the side of his head,[19] and then at once men seemed to know where they were going. He was knocked aside and lost Roach and Scotty and the others that he knew. It was a wild business, like a dream in which no one seemed real any longer. Across the road men were stripping palings from the fence of a church to fight with and from the side streets they were gathering stones. The white horse of the mounted policeman reared up as it was struck, unseating him so that he fell into the mob and was lost to sight. Johnson saw the police go back or down; two that were near him were driven back and one fell against a shop wall, hit with a stone that drew blood. Men were left where they fell and stopped fighting. Violence was new to these people so that they wanted results and not mob murder, but Johnson saw a woman kick someone as he fell, screaming in her anger all the time, and a man near him, his face all running with blood, shouting: "Get them—get them." He saw one of the police, red-faced and angry, driving in at a man who collapsed in front of him, while somebody else tried to catch the policeman's arm.

After that the shop-windows began to go, first with stones

19 his head] the head

and then with a long rake of the fence palings. The fight turned from the hall, no longer a fight, and the men who led it went back down the main street with their palings. They had tried to enter the hall and had been stopped. Now they no longer wanted to go inside. They were outside in the streets and had won their fight and were free from restraint. They were the swift runners and the leaders who went first and broke everything they saw without caring. To them it was the releasing of accumulated desire, a payment for the long weeks and months of monotony and weariness and poverty and anxiety that could be satisfied like this in a few moments of freedom and destruction.

Johnson went with them to the sound of glass breaking and women shrieking until he came to like it; past two men breaking a bottle of gin snatched from a hotel window over a lamp-post as they fought for it, and a woman stumbling back with her hand to her head; falling over a man who lay half on the pavement and half on the road saying "Christ, Christ," to himself, and then swearing, too, because he had to say something; turning to see whether he could stop and know what was happening and then being driven forward again, knowing that it no longer mattered what happened while the whole street moved forward with him; until suddenly it ended because the street ended. If the street had never ended, if it had gone on, instead of ending in the sea-front as it did, it seemed to Johnson as if he would still be moving with them and the plate glass would still be falling[20] as they went. At the end of the street the wave spent itself and recoiled.

Turning back up the street they could see for the first time the damage that had been done. Shop windows were

20 still be falling] be still falling

gone down both sides and the street that had been filled with marchers and onlookers was now broken into small groups of fighting, gesticulating people. What followed after the first rush was, by comparison, small and dirty. Those who fought by the windows for what they could take were not the real fighters, but the scavengers, not the front line, but the trailings and conscripts. Johnson, coming back up the street and feeling again a single man who could see and judge things for himself, saw a little jeweller who must have lived above his shop and come down to protect it, driven in by women who cursed him as they beat at him. His small, kind, Jewish little face was sweating and fearful. Then Johnson was wedged by an arcade entrance where a great gaunt man reached into a window for armfuls of cigarettes which he threw to the crowd, shouting and laughing as he did it. The man was drunk with excitement, blood streaming from a cut over his eye. Then, when he could not reach enough, he broke more glass and got inside the window and shovelled cigarettes out with his feet so that boxes and packets spilled out on to the pavement before anyone could catch them and a little bent woman, trying feverishly to gather them up, was knocked forward so that her head came onto the jagged glass and she fell face downwards with a cry that was lost in the shouting and raving of the big man inside the window.

The movement of men with him swung Johnson away from there and up the street again. It was curious to him at this moment, as the crowd rushed from place to place, to feel himself coming back again and to know what he himself was doing. He could see the same feeling grow on men's faces as they looked at one another, and wondered suddenly who was watching them at what they did, and knew that they themselves as single men were breaking and looting and no

longer all together. It was going to become important soon for
them to look after themselves and then the street would begin
to clear.

In one of the last rushes before this happened Johnson,
pressed into a throng near the top of the street, saw that it
was not loot that had brought this shouting, hooting mob of
men and women together, but an attempt at an arrest. The
police were re-forming and working from the head of the street
down, as in a battle, to retake it. A police sergeant, who must
have arrived late with reinforcements, for he was untouched,
and a plain-clothes detective held one man in a shop doorway,
and round them, like baying dogs who would nevertheless not
come within striking distance, pressed the crowd. They were
not yet willing for the return of everyday law and order and
for the taking of one of their number like this. The prisoner
behind in the grip of the sergeant struggled to get free and,
as Johnson watched, the sergeant raised his fist and bringing
it short round in a half-arm blow struck the man on the side
of his face so that he stood half-dazed and would have fallen
had he not been held up by the grip on his collar. His head[21]
dropped forward and Johnson saw then that it was Scotty.

As Johnson pressed into the crowd struggling towards the
doorway, there was a new shout from them in anger at the blow
and a new surge forward. But it stopped with the detective
in front of the sergeant and his prisoner, and one hand in
his pocket, shouting "Stand back or I'll shoot." The crowd
dropped back again uneasily so that Johnson, still pushing his
way forward, came in front facing the detective. Johnson was
angry now. He was angered by the brutal blow he had seen,
in all that evening's brutality, and angered, too, to think that

21 His head] He

of the few who would be picked out and punished for all that night's work, one of them must be Scotty, the small, the stupid, at heart the inoffensive.

A woman screamed hoarsely beside him: "They don't carry guns," and hoping this might be so, not really caring, he went in. The detective's hand came out of his pocket, clenched, and without a gun. Johnson going in towards Scotty went past the blow that came at him, but tripped as the detective's foot shot out and half fell. The same rush carried him to the sergeant who had his back half turned holding Scotty. Johnson drove one fist into the small of the sergeant's back, the other going high swung catching him on the side of his face.

In the red, angry face that turned to meet Johnson's attack, looking down at him, for the sergeant was a big man and heavily built, the main emotion was incredulity and surprise that anyone could hit him. It must have been a long time since anyone had hit this officer. His left hand still held Scotty by the collar. As he swung round Scotty was pulled between them and flung against the other side of the doorway. The sergeant's right hand coming low drove into Johnson, winding him. The sergeant dropped Scotty, who fell half forward and then was held by the crowd, and the sergeant with his face pressed close to Johnson hit with both fists into his body again; and Johnson, feeling behind him a blow from the detective that only grazed the side of his head, struck upwards and hit the sergeant below his chin. There was no longer surprise in the sergeant's face, but only anger, and as they stood, jammed now with the press as the crowd closed in, their faces almost touching so that for the moment neither of them could move, he said to Johnson: "I'll get you for this."

Then the crowd, pressing and shrieking, swung them together out of the doorway. Scotty disappeared. In the mêlée of the pavement the sergeant still had one arm holding Johnson by the right shoulder of his coat and, as Johnson tugged to pull away, the sergeant's fist came over in a last blow that caught him just above his eyes and knocked him back into the crowd on the street. Then the sergeant was back again against the wall, his helmet gone, his lip bleeding, waiting for what would happen while the crowd turned away down the street.

There was a new movement downwards again, driven by the pressure of new forces at the top, and the streets at the head were beginning to clear. The stream turned again towards the sea-front and Johnson went with it, half-dazed, shambling where before he had run, his breath gone, his stomach sick, and blood from the blow over his left eye running down his face. The rush of men and women, feeling fears of arrest for the first time, some of them stopping to snatch from windows as they went, but the main body going down the centre of the street, carried him with it until at last he came to the dark and comparative peace of the deserted wharf-head, and there he clung to the iron railings to support himself and was violently sick.

Chapter **VII**

Johnson came to himself again, leaning still sick and breathless against the wharf gates, trying to feel strength in his legs, to remember what had happened, and what he should do now. He could feel blood still running, though less freely, down his left cheek, and put up one hand to feel the swelling above his eye. It was swollen badly and tender to touch but he judged not seriously cut. He wiped some of the blood away with his handkerchief and smoothed his hair down so that it partly covered the bruise. His hat was gone and a pocket of his coat was torn open. When he had done that and could stand again he started to walk back along the road that ran by the wharves to where the lorry and his friends would be.

The town seemed much quieter now, if it were not just the contrast of the half-empty streets with the roar and singing that was still in his ears. The clock on the ferry buildings[22] chimed the half hour. He looked up. It was half-past ten. He had last thought of the time when the same clock struck seven as they were marching to join the procession. He must have been a long time by the wharf gates so that the cold he felt running through him was not unreal. As he passed the foot of the main street, walking on the far side and away from the town, he looked up it to see what was still happening there. It was very quiet now, though even from where he stood he could see light catching on broken glass strewn across the street and the shop windows that he saw were gaping and glassless. It was a clean business of wrecking that his friends had made.

He stopped waiting in the shadow which a corner of the

22 buildings] building

ferry building made and looked carefully ahead to where he
had to pass the bright light of the street lamps that were still
shining. Little groups of people were standing on street corners
talking anxiously; others were wandering up the centre of the
town like sightseers in a ruined city. And, what he didn't like,
police were about again, and what seemed to be special patrols
already, men in white armbands pacing up and down in front
of the broken shop-windows. Some of them carried rifles.
Ahead of him they had drawn a line across the road to the
west and were searching people for loot as they went past it. He
waited a moment uncertainly and then walked forward.

He had gone only a few yards in the bright light when he saw
two men watching him from the other side of the road. One of
them pointed to him. He recognised him by his build. It was
the police sergeant whose fist had cut open his eye. The sergeant
had found a helmet again which tilted forward strapless, over
a rough white bandage; he had with him a special constable, a
young man. As Johnson looked at them they moved forward
towards him. He waited a moment, uncertain whether it was
towards him or not that they were coming, and then, as they
quickened to a half-run, saw that they were. His legs were stiff
and weary, his head still ached, and his stomach was sick. He
turned and ran.

They did not follow him for long as he went back towards
what seemed like welcome darkness. He heard their footsteps
halt, and, looking round, saw them standing in the middle
of the road looking after him. He slowed again to a walk and
saw the special constable leave the sergeant and, crossing over
to the far side of the road again, come hurrying along towards
him. Johnson broke into a run again. The line was not drawn
so closely to the east. He saw someone from the other side of
the road run half-way across in an effort to cut him off and he

heard a whistle blow that might have been for him. But there
was too much still going on and too much disorder for them to
have time to attend to every man that ran. Bending forward,
his arms swinging, catching his breath in great sobs, he ran
into the darkness.

When he stopped again he was in darkness by the far
breakwater a good mile from the town. It was off here that he
and Petersen had brought the *Sea-Spray* to its last moorings;
he could see, looking out now across the harbour, the shape of
hulks breaking the sky. He felt better now, weary and still tired
in every part of his body, but clearer-headed with the cool night
air. Cars were going along the main waterfront road, hurrying
into town, with anxious property owners or the merely curious.
The outer suburbs of the city were mobilizing. He smiled to
himself, watching them without resentment. They could do
that if they wanted to. He rested, taking his breath.

It was not long before he grew cold again and, with the
cold, stiffness returned to his legs and the throbbing to his
head. He would have to move on, but first of all he felt through
his pockets and found his tin of tobacco and papers. He rolled
himself a cigarette clumsily in the darkness and smoked it
carefully between thickened and dry lips while he made his
plans.

He knew certainly now that he would not go back to the
camp. For the future and for what would happen in this city he
did not know; he did not care. There might be more troubled
evenings in the town, more rioting, more looting; they would
have[23] the soldiers out, the navy, the territorials; more shops
broken, more bandaged heads. In the pain of his head was
warmth and pleasure, and a good feeling running in his

23 they would have] and they would have

arm, remembering the surprised look that had come over the sergeant's face and the way his head went back. But, whichever way it went, it was no longer his fight and he did not care. The forces of disorder could not win; they could express themselves, but while they existed in disorder, they could gain nothing. It was possible that if he went back to the camp, walking through the night, no one would search for him, and he would pass unnoticed while things settled down into the slow running of the depression. He did not mind the police, but he wanted now neither a term in gaol nor a further term in relief camp. He had seen enough of cities and clay roads and camps, and the communal life of disheartened men. There was no life here either on relief or on riot. He would go away.

He felt in his breast-pocket, using his left hand with its sore knuckles tenderly. The little money that he carried and slept with was still there intact in its leather purse. He had twenty-four shillings—no railway fare for the distance he wanted to go—and, in any event, he judged it better not to travel openly with his clothes and his broken head telling their story. Behind him were the lights on the water[24] of ferry boats and harbour traffic and beyond the Rangitoto beacon winked steadily. There was a way of travel there, perhaps, but it was hard to get aboard ships and, besides, on the surface of the water was the ripple of a cool wind that made it look chill with winter. Over in front of him, not far away, were the railway station and the main railway yards, apparently still working normally with huge arc lights and sparks going up into the air from glowing bunkers. He stretched himself stiffly and smoothed his torn jacket down. He would go away.

24 on the water] *all previous edns read* of the water

Chapter VIII

Only after he had been in the truck for some hours did he wish that he had risked the lights of a station coffee-stall to get something to eat. It was bitterly cold and the stench of fertilizer, with which the truck was filled, blinded and choked him. He shifted two sacks again, grunting with the effort, to make room for himself between them, and pulled tight the tarpaulin which he had loosened to get in so that only his face was open to the air. The train moved uneasily along. He dozed fitfully in half-dreams that were filled with breaking glass and men fighting over him.

He was wakened finally with the train stopping. It had been held up before, once, at a junction just outside Auckland, but now, listening, he could tell that the trucks were being shunted off the line to come to rest with a jar of grinding brakes. He waited to see what would happen and heard voices and steps going down the line. Two men passed close underneath him so that he could see the glimmer of a lantern going past him and away in the distance and then quiet. He waited a few minutes longer, then lifted the tarpaulin carefully.

The night was breaking; he could see already a greyness in the east and the outline of trucks and station buildings growing sharper against the sky. There was a keenness in the air and a cleanliness that his cold body felt gratefully. He did not know where he was, one of the mining towns south of Auckland perhaps. Wherever it was, it was not far enough. He slid quietly out from under the tarpaulin and lowered himself gently to the ground. Then he stood, pressed against the truck, and replaced the tarpaulin so that no one noticing it would be on the look-out for a thief or a vagrant. Brushing the fertiliser dust from his clothes and hair he felt aching in him the hurts of the night's fighting and travelling, his head throbbing inwardly seemed to press outwards upon the bruised skin. He was tired and still sleepy, his mouth dry and parched. He followed the track cautiously back towards the lights of the station, his feet stumbling over the edges of sleepers that jutted on to the track, and stopped where a canvas boiler-filler hung down to drink gratefully a few drops of stale water.

Then he saw what he wanted. Nearer to the main line, and probably ready for pulling out, stood a line of trucks, cattle-trucks, for the most part, with one or two covered vans in the middle. He crossed over to it quickly, keeping in the shadows that were cast by the station lights a hundred yards in front, and tried to read the white chalk markings on the trucks that would tell him where they were bound for. It was hard to make anything out in the half-darkness and he was not willing to risk a match. 'Palmerston', two of them said. If he was lucky they were going there, a long way to the south. Some of the trucks were filled with cattle, moving uneasily. If he was unlucky, they were waiting for daylight to be unloaded; he would have to risk that. He listened, his ear pressed against one of the covered vans. It was empty. If he was still lucky, it had come from the Wairarapa or the Bay and was going home again. He opened the door and climbed warily in. After the sharp chemical dust of blood and bone mixture, the smell of straw, which lay over the floor of the van, was sweet. He curled himself up in one corner and went to sleep.

When he woke again it was with the jolt of the train starting, and for a moment his eyes wandered trying to place his surroundings. It was broad daylight now and his eyes took in at last the grey planking of the van. Then he turned on one elbow, feeling his stiffness and re-collecting himself again, and saw that he had company.

At the end of the box, surrounded as he himself was by a pile of damp straw, sat another man, an old man with close-cropped grey hair, and a gaunt unshaven face on which the white stubble showed. He looked like an escaped convict, with his grey flannel shirt and blue dungarees. Around him were spread his belongings, strewn from a canvas kit-bag, clothes, boots, two black tea-billies, a shirt, a khaki scarf, and a grey blanket. The old man sat in the midst of this, sightless and uncaring, swaying gently with the motion of the train. He held in one hand a black, unlabelled bottle, and while he rocked backwards and forwards his lips moved as if in prayer.

Johnson got up and shook the straw from himself, then, leaning one hand against the side of the car to steady himself, walked towards him. The old man looked up without emotion.

"Good day, brother," he said.

He tilted the bottle upwards and swallowed, straining the bony muscles of his neck. When he lowered the bottle he did not offer it to Johnson, but holding it tightly, and not looking at him, but towards the floor, said:

"Brother, you and I are brothers. That is all we know now, brother."

Johnson put down one hand from above him and took the bottle. The gnarled fingers closed on it despairingly, but once it had gone the old man did not move or protest, but sat, his eyes still on the floor.

"Where is Christ now?" he said. "Where is Christ now, where is Christ now, and where is Calvary?"

Johnson, braced against the wall which seemed to be rocking more violently, swallowed two mouthfuls of raw whisky. It was a cheap spirit that burned his throat and made him choke. He took a deep breath and drank again. Then he gave the bottle back to the old man who clutched it sightlessly.

"Mother Mary," he said. "Mother Mary. Where is Christ now, where is Christ now and His good men?"

Johnson sat down beside him, trying to catch the focus of his glazed eyes. His close-cropped head, the tight skin on his cheeks, gave him the look of an old and evil toad.

"Have you anything to eat?" Johnson asked him.

"I tell you, brother," said the old man "this is the end of the good things you and I know, the end of them now."

Johnson was searching in his kit, at first fruitlessly. At last he found what he wanted, a half loaf of white bread wrapped in newspaper inside one of the tea-billies. He broke it and ate hungrily.

"This is the end, brother," the old man said tonelessly. "This is the end. Where is Christ now? There are no men with us, no good men now, no Seddon, no Massey. There is no Christ, no Calvary. They are not with us."

He broke off and, as if observing Johnson for the first time, laid one lean hand on his knee.

"You are a good man, I can see that," he said. "I could be content then with one good man and Christ."

Johnson, filled for the moment with dried bread, leaned across and took the bottle from him again. It was now less than half full. He took two mouthfuls before giving it back. The old man had withdrawn his hand again from Johnson's knee.

"There is no peace now," he said, "no peace on earth. I knew Absalom, O Absalom, and Seddon, I knew Seddon. There are no more now, no more."

Johnson went back to his own end of the truck and, rolling himself a cigarette, watched the old man. He took one more drink, and then, corking the bottle solemnly, for which Johnson was glad, put it aside; he unrolled his blanket laboriously, and, wrapping himself in it, lay down and seemed to sleep.

The train moved south slowly all through that day. It waited three hours at what Johnson thought must be Te Awamutu, another three at Taumarunui. Each time it stopped Johnson got up and stood ready to jump out if anyone came along; but though they shunted some of the trucks once, the centre part of the train and the vans were not touched. The old man woke up once in the afternoon, walked across to the corner of the box and relieved himself, and then lay down again. Night came on as the train took its slow way, climbing through the bush-hills to the high plateau that runs across the centre of the island to the three snow mountains. The air grew colder and a steady rain was falling on the roof. Johnson, remembering the line, felt the curve of the spiral as the train climbed, and felt it straighten out again as it reached the plains. If it stopped again now, he was ready. It went on across the tussock flat and then started to go down into the valley beside the mountain, and as it slowed he saw the lights of a town that must be Ohakune.

He struck a match and bent over the old man, who still slept, breathing heavily. He seemed to Johnson to be well provided and well enough inured to small adversities. Johnson picked up his cloth cap and put it on; it would hide the ugly bruise that still showed on the side of his head. He took the woollen khaki scarf and wound it round his neck, turning up his coat collar to keep off the rain that was beating on the roof. He would have taken the old man's raincoat as well, but the old man slept in it and it would be difficult to remove without waking him. The train slowed to a halt. Johnson moved quickly to the door and as the brakes screeched jumped out on to the track, falling forward heavily on to his hands and knees. The momentum carried him forward and down a bank into long wet grass. The train had drawn in near the centre of the small station and there seemed to be lights on all sides. After waiting a moment he began to crawl along in the shelter[25] of the bank. Looking back he saw a guard walking with a lantern down the outside of the track coming from the engine. The door of the truck, which he had not had time to shut, swung half open, and he saw the lantern stop beside it. He was sorry to think that the old man's night should be disturbed in this way, but he could not stop to watch. He walked on down the line until he came to a bridge which ran above the road. He climbed over the edge, for it was without railings, and dropped ten feet into the road below. Then he picked himself up and, hurrying to get out of the rain, walked back into the town.

There seemed to be no place open where he could get a meal and the hot food he wanted so badly, and, after wandering around for a few minutes, he took his way back to the station. There he saw his goods train still halted by the side and apparently waiting for the arrival of a through express from the south which came in as he got to the station. Johnson drank coffee and ate sausage rolls at a counter crowded with travellers using a ten-minute break. They were from all points south and mostly going to Auckland; they talked, anxious for news of how things were going in the city.[26] "My God," said one man, coming in, "I've just been ringing through and they're at it again." They made way for this man and plied him with questions that he could not answer. Johnson, watching them, wondered if they were worried about their businesses or their wives and children. They talked as if they were going into a war area. Listening, he considered the necessity which all men have of dramatizing themselves. Then the train pulled out

25 in the shelter] the shelter
26 going in the city] going on in the city

and he was left finishing his second cup of coffee in front of a tired and irritated waitress, who watched him suspiciously. He pulled his cap further down over his eyes and went out along the platform to the waiting-room.

There was a fire there and two signalmen, sitting in front of it, talking of the latest news. "It's a proper dust-up," one of them said. "Well, you could've guessed it was coming," said the other. "Human nature won't stand the way things have been, no, it won't," and they agreed on that. Johnson got as near to the fire as he could and lay down on one of the wooden benches. He was ready to sleep again. About an hour after he had settled himself he was woken by the door opening and someone else coming in. It was the old man from the train. He carried his kit-bag over his shoulder, his grey blanket under one arm, the bottle sticking from his pocket. He did not seem to notice Johnson nor recognize his cap or scarf, but sat down on the opposite side of the room and, watched by the signalmen who turned round to look at him, drank the last drops[27] from his bottle. The old man seemed to have slept enough for the time. He remained sitting upright, his lips still moving quietly as he talked to himself. When Johnson woke up again in the early hours of the morning the old man had gone.

Johnson woke with the fire dying and the waiting-room empty, and the chill air of the morning coming in. Going outside he could see that the sky had cleared and now caught for the first time, rising above him, the white snow that was Ruapehu, the mountain of the plains. It rose up, nine thousand feet high, above the little township of timber mills and dairy factories. Below the snow-line came dark bush that ran down steeply to the edge of the town, and looking westward was flat

27   the last drops] the last few drops

that ran into bush hills as the country dropped again. In the cold of early morning the land looked cheerless and the bush heavy, dripping with the rain of the last night.

Johnson waited in the fireless waiting-room until the sun should come up and warm the air; about eight o'clock he found a small café that gave him breakfast of bacon and eggs and tea. He paid two shillings for this and bought some more tobacco, so that he had just one pound, which he put carefully away. Then he set off to walk, going westward, away from the mountain. It was still clear, though with drifting clouds and a cool wind coming from the south and west, but there seemed to be little alive or moving in the country that he passed, and the few small farms were uninviting. One or two cars passed him, but none offered a lift. It was still too near to[28] the towns for the real hospitality of the road. He came to a small town of more dairy factories and bought some bread, which he ate walking, and went on out of the town still going westward.

Early in the afternoon the driver of a cream-lorry called to him, passing, and he ran after it.

"You going far?" said the driver. He was a dark, thickset, swarthy man with no hat, and a head going bald backwards from his forehead.

"Looking for work," Johnson told him.

"You'll go far in this part of the world, mate," the lorry driver said. "You better jump in. One part of the country's as good as another for what you're doing."

Johnson got in and they drove on. Johnson said, shouting above the roar of the engine and the rattle of empty cans in the back and loose metal on the road:

"Things bad round here?"

28 near to] near

"Not too good, mate. Not too good. They ain't been worse as far as I can remember."

After a while the lorry driver said:

"More trouble in Auckland last night, they tell me, the bastards."

"What happened?"

"Tell me more windows broken though not so bad—soldiers out. Guess they'll have to be shown again the way they were in 1913, that's all. I was in that. I was in Hamilton then, just before the war it was. I tell you we was out and down in the wharves before sun-up with guns and all, no trouble at all. Loaded the bloody ships ourselves we did."

He spat over the side. Johnson was rolling a cigarette.

"Can I roll one for you?" he asked.

The driver nodded and so Johnson did this, and after lighting it, handed it to him. He had heard the story of the dockers' strike of 1913 before. It was a long time ago.

"What's behind all this trouble now?" Johnson said, making conversation.

"What's behind it? Why, hell, it's the same old trouble, ain't it? You're a farming man, ain't you? Bastards in town always had a good time—always wanting something more, more wages, shorter hours—makes me sick. Anyone ever worry how long the farmer works? Now things aren't so good in town and they don't like it. What d'they do? They listen to a lot of reds, a lot of bloody agitators. If they ain't Russians, they're Australians. That's what the trouble is."

"The farmer's not too well off, eh?"

"You're right, he's not. He's bloody badly off. What'd we get round here for a wool clip last year? Not enough to pay for taking it off the place. The wool-sheds are full of it, last year's, the year before's. Jesus."

"There's something a good deal wrong, you can see that," Johnson said. They were travelling along over desolate country where the great bush-fire of the early 'twenties had been. Blackened trees still standing, blackened, unrotted logs on the ground gave the hills the derelict air of a battle-field.

"There's something a good deal wrong, all right," the lorry driver said. "It's this bloody Government."

"It's a farmers' Government, isn't it?" Johnson said.

"Farmers' Government, my—," the lorry driver said. He seemed to like talking. "It's a bloody bankers' Government, that's what it is. If they'd take hold of the banks and make 'em do the work we want, now that'd be talking. Listen, everybody's had a cut, haven't they, one way or the other? Well, have the banks cut their wages?"

"I don't know."

"You can bet your boots they haven't. That's what we want then, ain't it? Just the right to control our money. Take over our banks, we'd be all right then. Now I'm no politician, mind you, but that's the way it seems to me. Control the money, we'd be all right. Mind you, I'm not one of these reds, don't go thinking that way of me. I just want money to do its work the way it ought to do."

The lorry slowed to a stop at a corner where a man stood waiting.

"This'll be Stenning," the driver said. "You'll have to ride in the back, mate, if you're going on. I promised I'd pick him up."

"Who's Stenning?"

"He's got a farm round here."

Stenning was a little man, shorter than the lorry driver, who was not tall, a man of about forty-five with grizzled fair hair. The thing that was striking about him was the great thickness and strength of his forearms and legs. He had light blue eyes that did not look directly at anything. He watched Johnson curiously as he got down and went round to the back of the van. Johnson got inside and travelled jammed up against rattling cans that slid backwards and forwards as the lorry took the corners. They were going down-hill now, leaving the plain that ran right across to the foot of the mountain. It was the same fire-swept, devastated country, broken and seamed, and showing clay where dry weather had caught it and cracked it. Johnson, observing it, felt tired and dispirited.

When they stopped at a cream-stand a little farther on, the lorry driver leaned on the back for a moment before taking out the can that Johnson passed to him.

"This Stenning says he might have a job for you," he said. "You better talk to him."

Johnson got down and went round to the front of the van.

"Tell me you might have a job?" he said.

Stenning looked at him for a moment without speaking. His was not an unpleasant face except for the very light blue eyes that turned, making him look a little shifty or mean. They took away from the strength of his body and made him seem uneasy.

He asked Johnson: "You used to farms? Can you milk?"

"Sure. I can milk."

"Where you come from last? You know anything about sheep?"

"Down south, Masterton way," Johnson said. "I've been on sheep farms."

"I got a job," Stenning said, "but there'll be no wages, not to speak of. You know what I took off of my farm last year? Fifty-two pounds. I can keep you in tobacco, some money if we make it. It's not a big farm."

"How big?"

" 'Bout fifteen hundred acres. I got eight hundred sheep, ten cows, a few horses."

"I'll take it," Johnson said.

They shook hands solemnly. The lorry driver, who had joined them and stood stolidly listening, said:

"It's as good as you'll get, mate. You could do worse with things the way they are."

"You got any gear?" Stenning asked him.

"I left it down south," Johnson said. "I'll get it sent on." He climbed into the back of the lorry and they drove on. At the next stop the lorry driver paused again as he lifted a can out and said:

"You won't be doing so bad, mate. This Stenning's not a bad fellow."

"He seems all right to me," Johnson said.

"They say he's a bit mean—reckon he's a good farmer," the lorry driver said, and lifted the can out on to the stand. He came back again.

"He's got a half-caste wife," he said.

"What of it?"

"Nothing. She's a bitch, that's all."

"He got any children?"

"Nope. He ain't got any children. He ain't been married so long, a year or a bit more. She was well known around here, she was." He grunted to himself and walked back to his seat in the front.

Two miles beyond that point they came to a cream-stand and letter-box where a small clay road turned off to the left to Stenning's farm, and Johnson and he got down. Johnson said good-bye to the driver.

"I'll see you around some time," the driver said. "Name's Sayers."

"Mine's Johnson."

"I'll be seeing you around." He started up the engine, then leaned out over the door again.

"You play football?" he shouted.

"No."

"Pity. We get up a team around here sometimes." He waved his hand and drove off. Stenning arranged the parcels that he had collected in two sacks and gave one to Johnson. They set off to walk down the clay road.

"It's a mile and a half," Stenning said.

The road ran sharply down-hill into a small valley. On both sides were dead trees and standing fern; little creeks bursting with the rains of the night before ran down from the hills; their feet splashed heavily through pools that had formed in the deep ruts of the road. Except for an occasional ewe nibbling at some odd patch of grass among the fern, there was no life and no sound except running water.

They walked on in silence at first and then Stenning talked a little about the riots. He summed it up finally:

"It's a damn' bloody hard country wherever you live in it," he said.

They came at length to the white gate of Stenning's farm. The clay road ran on past it, sunk low now in the valley. They went through the gate and up towards the small iron-roofed house that stood on a rise surrounded by paddocks that flattened out towards the river. Johnson could see that the green grass on these river flats was worth farming: it grew thick and heavy and clean. The dairy sheds and the yards and the wool-shed were farther down towards the river, and the cows from the field beyond had drawn in ready for milking. It was about five in the afternoon. As they walked up the track to the house a woman ran out from the front door, stood looking at them for a moment, and went in again.

"My wife, Rua," Stenning said. "You'll be sleeping in the *whare* down there," he said. "There's no room in the house." He pointed to a little hut that stood near the sheds.

Stenning's wife came out again and met them on the steps of the house. She was little more than a girl, perhaps twenty-two or three. She had been pretty not long ago; she was still pretty, though sulky and ill-tempered looking. She was not very dark, and her straight black hair, hanging down over one side of her face, showed off the deep olive pinkness of her cheeks that had grown a little too fat and rounded. She looked at Johnson curiously and rudely, without speaking. Stenning said:

"This is Johnson. He's going to stay and work awhile."

She turned and they followed her into the house. The table in the kitchen in front of the range was set for tea. She set another cup, banging it noisily on to the table, and took the tea-pot from the range. They ate tea and bread and butter while she asked Stenning what he had brought, jumping up to tip the sacks out and open the parcels on the floor. The house was crudely and amateurishly[29] built, unlined, and with newspaper for wallpaper pasted over the cracks of the weather-boarding. There seemed to be only three rooms and no bath-room. The house as a whole looked dilapidated and dirty. There were unwashed dishes piled in the scullery, the butter was badly made, saltless, and full of water. Johnson, helping himself to strong tea, felt gratefully the heat from the stove and the steam rising from his legs, wet after the road.

"You and I'll milk," Stenning said, when tea was over. Johnson nodded.

"You won't want me, eh?" Rua said, looking up. Her voice

29 amateurishly] *original read* amateurly

was pleasantly soft and curiously musical. The ill temper remained in her eyes.

"You can have a rest to-night," Stenning told her, and to Johnson: "Can I lend you some clothes?"

"What I have'll do," Johnson said, and looking down at them realized that they were in no good state for anything but the cow-yards. What had been a rough tweed suit, wearable in a city, was dirty and torn and still smelled of blood-and-bone. Rua was watching him curiously and he remembered, now that he was indoors and his cap off, the ugly bruise still showing on his forehead. He ran his hand over it gently and smiled.

"Fell off a train," he said, and getting up went out with Stenning down the track to the milking-shed.

Coming back to the house later after Stenning, who had left him to finish, carrying the buckets and separator parts to be washed, he heard Rua's voice arguing shrilly inside. She was saying:

"And who he is God knows, and you don't, and up to no good around here. But that doesn't matter to you that I've got enough work already without cooking and feeding for him as well. And I suppose you think there's enough food in this house for everybody?"

Stenning said something which he could not catch, and the buckets clanking on the gate that led into the yard at the back of the house stopped the conversation.

Johnson washed himself at the tank outside and sat on the steps watching the last of the light catch the snow on Ruapehu. He had seen the mountain before, but never at such close quarters as it was now in this part of the world. The glaciers rose up red and bloody to the peaks, that were clear against the sky, and below them was the dark line of bush and the shadow of the foot-hills. He did not seem to have moved far in his day's travel. The mountain towered up directly out of the country as it had seemed to do at the station in the morning. Near at hand to the house, bush came down almost to the yard at the back. It was quiet and heavy with night coming on. Bush-hens were calling across the valley and he could hear the hushed roar of the snow river going by. Johnson smoked a cigarette and stretched his tired legs gratefully. He sat there while the air grew dark and cold about him and then went into the kitchen. After supper he helped wash up the dishes and then went, with Stenning and a storm lantern guiding him, across the field to his *whare*. He slept well.

Chapter IX

After a few days Johnson wrote to Scotty asking him to send his things down if it wasn't difficult and if nobody cared where he was. He took the letter himself down to the corner one morning, when he went out with the cream cans on a pack-saddle, and gave it to Sayers, open, with two shillings to buy a money order to cover postage. His clothes came back in a week's time with a letter inside, but not from Scotty. It was from Robertson.

"Your things go to you herewith," he wrote, "minus, I'm sorry to say, your spare pair of boots, but one of the bastards took them just after you left us. You left pretty sudden though, didn't you. Scotty's been ill, he's in hospital. He came back that night looking bad, but it's not that really, it's the old trouble, his cough. He's in the big hospital in town. He was worried about you. No one else is worried about you. They've all got their own worries. I told the boss you'd gone to a job in the country. There's a few forms you should have filled in first. I shouldn't worry too much about that.

"I expect you read the papers so you heard what happened after you pulled out. I went into town myself the night after, the Friday night, just as an observer like. There was a big crowd out again at the top of the town waiting for something to happen but not so many ready to start it. They had a lot of "special constables" they call them out, boys from the colleges and all sorts, enough to make any one want to throw a brick, and some smart boys on horseback from the country having the hell of a good time riding about. It was quite like a circus for a while only the show never really got started.

There was some stones thrown and a few windows gone, but that was all. The police—the real police that is—were on top. They were getting a bit of their own back for the night before. Professional pride that's called. The next night there was some crowds about and one or two meetings there were over the week-end, but it didn't amount to a lot. The excitement's over for a while. The fellows here say it's enough for the present. That means they don't want any more, I guess, just now. I don't know. Maybe this'll frighten the Government into handing out a little more relief. It's food they want mostly for women and children in the towns, food in the country that produces it, mind you. Both sides are suckers. The fellows here are pretty proud of what they've done and the fine time they had. There was free cigarettes going about for a few days I can tell you. I tell them if they'd think a little more and organize and smash a little less they'd do better, but you can't put sense into their bloody heads, not in this country. They're too ignorant. It's enough to make you sick of it all, and now they're back on the pick and shovel life again like a lot of sucking pigs.

"It isn't all over yet a while just the same, I'm thinking. Maybe you won't notice things so much down where you are. It sounds a God enough forsaken hole. Somehow I don't think things will be quite as good again for a time to come, not to my way of thinking. This has brought too much out into the open that people didn't like to think about. It's like if you had a body in the cellar you didn't want known about and suddenly you found it laid out on the table when your friends went in to dinner. That's the way it is. As I figure it out, this used to be a fine easy country where everybody had money or could make it. Maybe there was a few that didn't, but there was enough having a good time to forget about the others.

It was dead easy then to be a pal to everybody and to crack hearty up and down the country. It was a nice small country too, a pretty nice little country. It's a bit different now. You can see fellows looking at each other when you go about in town, thinking maybe which side are you on, you bastard, maybe you're out to break a window, maybe you're a special constable on your night off. It makes a difference all right. Men don't talk so freely around the way they did. You can see the fellows here on the road now looking up when anybody goes by, like a gang of convicts waiting for a chance to throw a brick, which is what they're likely to be if the police ever get to checking up on the records of some of them.

"I reckon you were wise to get out of it when you did, son. This isn't a life here. I'll do the same soon, I'm thinking, only I'm getting a little old to be wandering the country. If they're wanting any good shepherds down there you could tell me, only remember, I don't milk cows and I'm not learning."

Johnson missed the end of it all except for what he got in the weekly when it came down, the court cases, the men in hiding, the ones that got six months and nine months and two years, the fellows with gelignite trying to blow up buildings. He missed all that and didn't mind. He wrote to Scotty at the hospital and got no answer, and had a card a month later from Robertson to say that Scotty was dead. So the only man he wanted to keep in touch with was dead, and he was glad to be back in the country and away from it all. It's the towns that play hell with men, he said to Stenning. The quiet of the country closed over him while he thought of it until the camp and the men in it, the streets and the lights of the city and the cold discomfort of the camp were farther from him than things that had happened years before.

Chapter X

The economics of Stenning's farm were simple.

"You see, Johnson," he said, "in a good year I used to make three to four[30] hundred from wool and lambs. I didn't use to keep cows except one or two running around near the house. Then I married Rua and she came and could help milk, and so I got the cows in to keep the house going. Used to drink condensed milk in the tea before then—by God, I'm not sure it wasn't a better life." He laughed at his joke. He didn't often laugh.

"Even now, with butter gone to hell the way it has, the cows still pay for most things. Wool ain't worth the trouble to send out. Lambs won't pay the mortgage. Besides, I've tried this[31] last two years to keep all the stock I could on the place, and you can't fatten spring lambs up here."

"You got a mortgage?" Johnson asked.

"Now who hasn't got a mortgage in this country?" Stenning said heavily.

"Can you pay interest on it these times?"

"Who the hell can? Nobody I know. And who cares? Do you?"

"What happens when it isn't paid?"

"Nothing happens. If everybody can't pay, nothing happens. It isn't like it was a few years ago; they sold me out of a farm after the war. Now they're damn glad to have me stay. Listen, when I moved in here three years ago the farm had gone to hell. I brought it round till it nearly looks like a farm again. They'll pretty near pay me to stay on."

30 three to four] three or four
31 this] the

Johnson considered the question.

"I guess that's all right," he said, "but it's different to owning your own land, isn't it?"

"I own it all right."

"Sure, you own it or they own it. It depends whether they like having you here or not."

"I own it all right."

"What about the stock?"

"They're on mortgage, too. The company stocked me up when I came in. I paid them off a bit. With stock prices the way they are now, if they sold me up they'd not get half of what's left back, not half of it."

"They won't sell you up?"

"Nope, they won't sell me up. If they sold up this place there'd be nothing left in the country that wasn't gone, sink and swim alike."

"Well, it's a case all right," Johnson said. "I guess it's all right. It's like working for someone else though, not for yourself."

"They're not a bad lot," Stenning said. "They haven't been bad to me. They're not so easy what stores they let in on the account, and for grass seed or harness, or a new draught horse, Gawd, you'd think you were crazy the way they look at you. But we ain't so bad. It's a living all right. You can still kill a sheep when you want some meat, only at that I don't go out of my way to ring them up and tell them about it." He laughed again.

"Still it isn't working for yourself though, eh?"

"Sure, they own it all, I suppose, if you look at it that way," Stenning said. "That goes for all the farms in this damn' country, don't it? Fair's fair. If they let me alone and we hold out through this spell, I'll get it off of them[32] yet. That's fair

32 off of them] off them

enough. Good times they make a bit. Bad times no one makes anything. That's how it is."

"It's a case all right," Johnson said. "When they send in the bill for back interest, that'll be a case."

"They won't do that," Stenning said. "There'd be a riot."

They were standing talking by the yard after milking, with the early morning sun rising and drying the dew on the grass.

"You always been farming?" Johnson asked.

"Ever since the war," Stenning said. "Before that cabinet making. Father was a cabinet maker. He was a German."

"You go to the war?"

"Sure, everybody went to the war, one side or the other. I was at Gallipoli."

"I've been knocking round on this game ever since the war myself," Johnson said. "I never tried for a farm of my own.'

"You should've done. It's a better game than working for another man."

"You always been in this part, around here?"

"Nope—third farm this is. First was down in Nelson. Couldn't grow fruit trees. Second was near here. I'll own this bloody piece of land before I die."

They spent a day riding round it. Stenning seemed to like Johnson to the extent of taking his work there seriously and trying to interest him in it. The best part of Stenning's farm was three horses that had been bred from good stock in the Wairarapa. They ran in the big log paddock with half a dozen Maori hacks of poor quality—brought in wild from the tussock plains, Stenning said—but the others could be told half a mile away by the way they carried their heads.

Stenning rode a great white mare called Jonquil, Johnson a wicked, quick-footed little horse that picked its way over logs and up hill tracks like a dancer. They rode up and down the gullies, looking at the patches of grass where it grew in 'biddy-bid' and fern.

The farm ran along one side of the valley with the river at the bottom for a boundary, and across the river the banks rose sharply in heavy bush.

"That's a bit the fire missed," Stenning said, as they went past it, along the river flats. "There's the remains of a farm over there."

It was true, though all Johnson could see was a corner of the iron roof of the house between trees. The fields that had been cleared were smothered head-high in fern and scrub.

"There used to be a swing bridge across here," Stenning said, "the wire's still there. Fellow got killed in the war, I think. It's not been farmed since."

They rode on past the bridge and took a track that ran up a ridge to the top of the valley, and then along a farther track that took them to Stenning's boundary. There was high fern on beyond this, too, and trees growing up again.

"This next bit ain't farmed either," he said. "Was cleared once a long way back by two young fellows from England. One of them got left some money so they gave it up. It's a nuisance not having no neighbour. Means you keep all the fences up. All the weeds and such grow alongside of you. There was a lovely crop o' ragwort there this year. Still it means you don't lose any sheep except from natural causes."

They turned their horses looking down the valley to the river.

"I want to fence this off in three parts," Stenning said. "That's why I wanted some help in. If they give me time and some fencing wire, and maybe a bit of grass seed, we'll get it done. Then when I burn and sow it I can turn stock on to it that'll eat the fern down as it grows. Give grass a chance, that's what they say, and it'll beat the fern. That's the winter's work."

They rode down again and back along the flats to the house.

It was a hard winter and a colder part of the world than Johnson could remember. Farther down the valley, they told him, it grew warmer, and the land was better. Up at the head of it, on Stenning's land, the frosts came down at night so that the tank froze and even the pools on the edge of the river were covered over with ice. In July there was snow falling and though it did not lie with them round the house it stayed on the hill-tops all around and covered Ruapehu down below the bushline. Through June, July, and August there was rain, caught by the mountain so that it seemed to fall endlessly, week after week.

The cows dried off, so that there was little milking to do, but Johnson and Stenning worked days that were longer than ever and hardly shortened by dark, running fences from the boundary line on the ridge down to the river. There were trees to fell first to clear the line, and logs to be sawn and split for posts, and then, when the line was clear, the fencing began. Johnson and Stenning rode out each morning. Even when it rained and the days were dark and driving, Stenning would get up after breakfast from the table and, coatless, since it didn't matter what one wore when one worked in the rain, Johnson would follow him. They would bring in the horses and saddle them, and go off with cold tea and bread and cold mutton for lunch, and come home late in the afternoon, with night falling and a cold wind blowing off the glaciers into their faces, so that the horses turned away from it and went unwillingly through the mud and logs.

The two men grew to respect each other in this work. Johnson could not like Stenning, he was too sullen and unattractive a man, but he liked working with him. He admired his great forearms and his skill with an axe, and the way he drove at the work in a fury of accomplishment. He was good towards Johnson and treated him equally and fairly. When they first went out in the bad days of rain and snow he made it so that Johnson seemed to come of his own accord because he could not leave Stenning to work alone. They worked without talking except sometimes as they ate, and then little; they would work sometimes half a mile apart and not meet all day until Johnson would hear Stenning call and look up to see him leading the horses over for the home ride.

On good days, when the sun shone and the ground perhaps was hard and sharp with frost, it seemed the best life in the world. Then they could light a fire for lunch and heat up the black tea, and grill chops on sticks over the fire. Then Ruapehu would shine in the sun so that the black rocks and the hummocks in the ice were plain to see and the green on the glaciers, and below the bush would be blue with haze. Johnson would sit, his back against a log, rolling a cigarette after lunch, and watch the mountain, fascinated by its whiteness.

"Did you ever climb that mountain?" he asked Stenning once, remembering how he had looked at it before with Scotty.

"God no, now what would I be doing that for?" Stenning said. His eyes were running down the line of half-built fence. By August, when the first lambs came and Stenning had to ride round his flocks most of the days, they had one line down and another ready for wiring. It was a good winter's work.

Stenning said to Johnson one day in September:

"Johnson, why don't you settle here?"

Johnson grinned. "I'm not thinking of moving on yet awhile," he said.

"I didn't mean like that," Stenning went on, screwing up his face with the effort of concentrated thought. "What I was meaning is, why don't you have a stake in something here? You're still young, but you're getting older. How old are you?"

"I'm thirty-five."

"That's right. It's the time to stop wandering the country."

"What's the proposition?"

"Well, it's like this, if you like to stay on here and see through the bad time, things are going to turn."

"Who says so? Seems to me sometimes we've gone so far into this damned slump we'll never climb out again."

"Sure, things'll be all right again. They had worse than this before you and I were born. Now, listen, you know as well as I do there isn't any money going here now and you've worked as hard as I have on that basis. That's fair enough and we've made a good job of it. Now listen, if you'll stick it another year or two, taking what comes, and maybe nothing much will come, I'll cut you in on a third share of the place."

"It's a good offer," Johnson said.

"It'll be a good offer if things go right the way I reckon they will. If we can hold on here and not sell stock, but build it up and get the place cleared, we'll be sitting pretty when prices rise. What I'm thinking is this. If you take a share and work in here for two or three years we could take on one of these other farms as well. You could take Hathaway's across the river. It's got the same dairy flats as this place if they were cleared."

"I haven't any capital," Johnson said. "I couldn't take a farm."

"I never had any capital," Stenning said. "Not after the last time I walked off. You don't need capital. The company would stake you for that farm like a shot if times were better and if they knew your work."

"It's a good offer," Johnson said.

"Sure, it isn't a bad offer. I wouldn't make it if I didn't want someone that would work on here for damn and all these bad times. You undertake to stay on—that's the promise I want. I cut you in on a third share of whatever we make and in two or three years' time I back you for one of these farms. It would make the hell and all of difference to have them both cleared and working. We could shift the stock about on them both."

"You need a bridge to work Hathaway's," Johnson said.

"There's shallows half a mile down river where you can put sheep across. They only used the swing bridge, I reckon, for the house. We could put that up again."

"It's a good offer," Johnson said. "I wasn't wanting to move. I'll take it."

It was a verbal contract that they made and which neither of them considered necessary to put into writing. When Stenning made up accounts at the end of the year there was eighteen pounds due to Johnson for nine months' work, less tobacco and other things which he had had in on the stores' account. He took what was due to him and bought some whisky for Christmas, and banked the rest.

Chapter XI

Sundays were the worst days on the farm. Even Stenning did not work then, except to milk, and there was nothing to do for the three of them, Rua and Stenning and Johnson, but to sit about and wait for it to be Monday again. If it rained and they had to stay in the house all day, by the evening Johnson had had enough and would go back to his *whare* and lie there reading. It was a relief when Monday came and they could ride out again. Stenning never talked if he could help it, not even to Rua, and she would sit sulkily or play her few worn records on the gramophone until Johnson knew every scratch in them by heart. When Stenning swore at her, as he did, she would stop and get[33] them a meal, banging and clattering with pots and burning the food, as likely as not, and then they would eat, silently and bad-temperedly. Johnson himself found Stenning trying on days like this. He would sit for hours before the fire, neither moving nor speaking, perhaps playing with a sheath-knife,[34] sharpening it on the sole of his boot or carving wood shavings from a bit of firewood until the hearth in front of the range was littered with them. Then he would get up and perhaps look out of the window at the fields and the rain, grunt heavily to himself, and sit down again.

Johnson didn't like Stenning personally. He didn't blame Rua if she felt the same way towards her husband. He tried to imagine once what it must be like for her living with Stenning, and reckoned it probably wouldn't be the world of fun. Stenning himself never showed any tenderness towards her; what he did show was a good deal of ownership, but he

33 get] give
34 a sheath-knife] his sheath-knife

was tolerant enough and never interfered with what she did provided the milking was done and the shed kept clean, and the meals tolerably enough cooked and ready when they were wanted. Rua seldom looked happy. She dragged about the house, as a rule, in a soiled frock, the neck torn and open, her hair unwashed and uncombed, in down-trodden slippers. It wasn't all to be answered by her complaint that she never had a new dress or any new clothes since they were married. There wasn't any money to spare for anything except the necessities on Stenning's farm. When the lambing season came and Stenning was busy with his sheep, she and Johnson took on the milking again, and work of this kind she did fairly well. She milked well and, in spite of the fat lines of her face, was as strong as many men. She could lift the cans of cream up on to her horse for the ride to the corner without effort.

Johnson saw her happy only occasionally, when her friends and family would come over to visit her. They lived in a village on the site of an old *pah*, ten miles down the valley, and rode over sometimes on a Sunday to spend the day racing their horses up and down the fields and jumping logs, or sitting in the sun singing and talking. They were an odd, cheerful, shiftless lot, as careless as gipsies, and more temperamental. Rua's young brothers and cousins were smart young men who affected wide purple flannel trousers and broad-brimmed hats with coloured feathers in the band. The women were either ageing and fat and contented, or young and shy and perhaps pretty. They nearly all wore pink. They never came except in a large party with several children and baskets of food. Stenning never joined in the party, but sat and watched them with amusement, tolerantly enough.

"Them's my relations-in-law," he said once to Johnson, watching them in the fields. There were at least twenty of them.

"You've got plenty," Johnson said.

"You said it. There was a time when I first got married, seemed like they were all coming to live here. I reckon I stopped that. Now they get tea when they come over here and that's all. Don't seem to mind. They're not a bad lot."

Sometimes Rua's father, a wizened man, whose bloodshot eyes indicated an illicit source of drink in the dry King Country area, or one or two of the older men, would talk to Stenning, arguing volubly about the merits of horses or cows or ways of farming, and Stenning would listen and comment dryly without ever paying any real attention.

"They're damn' poor farmers," he said to Johnson. "The only thing they can grow's potatoes."

But Rua was really happy at these times. She ran and played with them all, and talked and laughed. It was obvious to Johnson that she made jokes with them about Stenning and himself, and once he saw her imitating Stenning, with his slanting eyes and rough, shambling walk, to an admiring group of children. If Stenning noticed this, he didn't seem to mind. His contempt for them all was too great. On days like this when they had gone, riding off in the late afternoon to milk their own cows, with a great deal of noise and shouting and probably four children on a starved Maori hack bringing up the rear, Rua would be more sullen and more restless than usual, and more careless of herself and of the house.

It was clear to Johnson, nevertheless, that she had advanced herself by marrying Stenning. Her friends and her family to whom she really belonged might laugh at Stenning. They probably despised him for marrying her, but Rua herself had gone up in the world. She had married a white man with a farm, and not a poor white either, who would one day come back and live in the *pah* with them, but a real white who worked and kept himself.

They had a good party with the family at Christmas-time. The year had gone by then and the summer had come in, slowly at first, with more rain through September and October, but by November it was hot and the fern was going brown on the hills. They sheared the sheep in November. Stenning did most of this while Johnson yarded and rolled and baled. Part of the clip went into the shed with last year's and part went out to the sales for what it would fetch. Then when the first dry weather came in December they burnt off the four-hundred-acre paddock they had fenced, sweating to keep the fire in line and away from the fences. Stenning could not buy enough seed to sow it all, but they scattered as widely as they could and turned stock on to it and trusted to luck. In those days, when the sun was at its height, it seemed to be hotter up on the hills than it had ever been anywhere else, even in the north. Ruapehu was dazzling white and the snow melting filled the river to its banks.

It was a good summer after a wet spring.[35] Johnson and Stenning cut the grass in the hay paddocks with a borrowed cutter before Christmas. "Last year," said Stenning, "it rained every other day till March, when it set in to rain perpetual-like. There wasn't any hay. There was just ensilage." Then, two days before Christmas, some of Rua's people came over to help with the hay-making. They camped in the wool-sheds and down by the river. The hay-making was something of a party which Stenning himself couldn't take seriously.

"These bloody cows," he said, "and this bloody hay. If I could afford to have just sheep, there'd be something to be said for the farming life."

35 a wet spring] the wet spring

It was hot down in the fields, hotter even than it had been up on the hills, where there was sometimes a little wind. Down below there was only the choking scent of hay and the glaze of the sun. The Maoris made a race of everything they did so that sometimes Stenning swore at them for missing corners or raking badly, but they worked hard. On Christmas Eve they worked on until dark, getting the last field gathered to leave them free for Christmas Day. There was still the clover paddock, but they left that, cocking it up in case of rain, and called it a day. Even at that Johnson couldn't sleep until late in the night with the singing and laughing and banging of doors that went on in the wool-sheds beside him. Christmas Day was all heat and laziness. There were cows to milk, but no other work was done. The whole party, up to nearly thirty, came over in the morning, and the women cooked dinner in the open down by the river, with fowls and hot hams and sweet potatoes sent down from the north. They lay about afterwards in the hot part of the day and Johnson swam with some of the boys in the river. In the evening there was beer and a dance in the wool-shed. It was the one party of the year and bad times would not stop it. Two Maoris had brought the beer in sixty miles by road, two great barrels on a dray covered with tarpaulin from the sun, and everyone turned out to welcome it. They cleared the wool-shed, stacking the bales round the sides so that the floor was an almost passable dancing floor, and everything rank with the rich greasy smell of wool. They sat round there as the sun went down and one of the Maoris— Tom Heeney, they called him, though that was not his real name, he was fat and called after the prize-fighter—played a concertina and they danced with others, riding in from miles around, and the first barrel of beer being opened with noise and excitement in the yards outside.

Johnson found Stenning up at the house and they sat there sharing the bottle of whisky which Johnson had brought with him. Rua's father and two others came in for a while. Rua's father talked a great deal, with reminiscences of older and better times to him, and a long story of his brother who had been killed in the Boer War. After a while he went to sleep with his head on the table, and Stenning finished his drink, putting down the china cup he drank from, and got up.

"I'm going to bed," he said. "Thanks for the drink," and went into his room.

Johnson went out and down to the wool-shed where the party was still going on. They gave him some beer in an empty tin that tasted of disinfectant and he sat watching them. After a while Rua stopped dancing to talk to him.

"Where's Bill?" she asked—meaning Stenning.

"He's gone to bed, went to bed an hour ago."

She shrugged her shoulders. "Can you dance?" she asked him.

"I can try," he said, and got up. She said something he did not understand to the young boy who had been her partner and danced with Johnson. 'Tom Heeney' was still playing his concertina. 'Moonlight and Roses' was his song and he played this over and over, singing it to himself. It was a long time since Johnson had danced, and he did not do it very well, but felt comfortable with the beer warming him on top of the whisky he had drunk. Rua laid her head on his shoulder while they danced and did not talk. There were not many other couples dancing. Rua's younger sister and a white boy, whom he had never seen, made one of them. Rua's sister was slight and pretty. She was pretty as Rua herself must have been not long ago, though she looked pretty this night with her hair done smoothly and a clean frock on. After a while

Johnson stopped, apologizing for himself and his dancing. Rua laughed and left him, going back to the young Maori boy who seemed to have been waiting for her, and Johnson sat down by the door again and let them fill his tin with beer.[36] Some of them were growing a little noisy and one boy was sparring in front of 'Tom Heeney', challenging him to fight. The big man stopped playing for a moment and pushed out his hand with the fingers extended, hitting the boy in the chest so that he staggered across the room and sat down heavily on a bale, while everybody laughed, and 'Tom Heeney' began playing again.

After that the evening grew quieter. Towards the end of it they were sitting around and singing. They sang 'Maori Moon', which was a song half-jazz and half-native, and sang it softly and sweetly. The lanterns inside threw shadows over them and the tired children sleeping, and outside, through the cracked boards, there was the glimmer of a harvest moon. Then they sang songs which were their own and which Johnson had never heard before, with Maori words and Maori rhythms, while he listened half drowsily until, growing sick with the beer he had drunk, he went out and walked up and down in the cool air away from them. He could still hear their voices clearly in the night. Some time after that the party broke up and men saddled their horses and rode home, though most of Rua's party slept by the river or in the shed. They were awake again when Johnson was getting the cows in at six o'clock, and when Stenning and he rode out later in the day they were packing up to go. The two men waved to them, saying good-bye.

"You couldn't stop them having a good time," Stenning said, "that you couldn't. Who'll pay for that beer of theirs,

36 with beer] of beer

nobody knows. They'll sell something; they'll pay for it all right. There's not one of them hasn't a store account for a hundred pounds or more. D'you enjoy the party?"

"It was all right."

"Rua seems to have enjoyed it, she ain't properly up yet. She said it was a good party. It's good for them to have a break like this once every year. It costs me nothing except a bit of time. It's going to be a scorcher again to-day." They rode on up the ridge, Stenning on his white mare ahead and Johnson's Darky going warily and neatly behind.

Chapter XII

The new year came in. Rua went away for the night to a dance somewhere to celebrate it, and after that came a hot January and February, and time to muster the sheep again for dipping. It was hard to tell what was happening in the country outside. Little news came into them and only stray bits of gossip. Prices had not risen and the country was as poorly off as ever only that it seemed better in summer for men who had no money and no homes but a camp. There was no end to the slump; there was no end that anyone could see. Men had got past the time when they thought how things would be once this natural calamity had passed. They had settled into an apathy which was not despair but resignation. To Johnson, living there, none of these things mattered any longer. Stenning thought and talked about them sometimes, understood the Government's moratorium which would ultimately settle the question of his unpaid interest and the mortgage on his farm; he argued, with no one contradicting him, questions of exchange and currency. But neither to Johnson nor to him were these things at all real. What was real was the battle they were both fighting with the land they worked. So long as they could live there and were left alone, it was a battle that they could carry on, even while the world sank outside them.

The small world in which Johnson lived might have gone on like this for a long time, but it broke unexpectedly. It was in February, just before they mustered the sheep for dipping. He was in bed one night sleeping, and it must have been about eleven o'clock and quite dark, when he was wakened by someone calling. What he heard was not just the sounds of loneliness which settled on the farm once the sun had set, the

116

bush-hens calling, or the native owl crying mournfully across the valley, or the sound of wind in rustling manuka. What he heard was more real and closer at hand. He turned over, still sleepily, and then was wide awake, listening. He heard Rua's voice again screaming shrilly from the house. He lay in bed wondering what he should do and then heard a door banging and the sound of footsteps running. The next moment Rua was hammering on the door of his *whare* and crying to him to let her in. He got out of bed and opened the door and she fell forward over the steps clutching at his knees. She was sobbing and held on to him so that it was difficult for him to move. He bent down and lifted her up.

"What's the matter?" he said sharply. "What's the matter?" and when she did not answer shook her roughly by the shoulders. After a while she got her breath and seemed calmer. He could not see her face. She said:

"He'll kill me. He said he'd kill me. He said he'd cut my throat."

"What's the trouble?" Johnson asked. "What's the trouble? What's it all about?"

She began to speak again, but her voice choked, and she would have begun to cry, but he shook her, still holding her shoulders with both hands. At last she said:

"He's a swine. He's a dirty swine. He'll kill me. I know he'll kill me."

Johnson said, talking to her quietly as to a child: "He won't kill you. Now, listen, he won't kill you. He wouldn't do anything like that. He's a good fellow. He wouldn't really hurt you. Now what's all the trouble anyway?"

She would not tell him but repeated: "He's a filthy bloody swine," yet she became calmer. He sat her down in the doorway and held her arm until she steadied herself and became quiet again. Then he said:

"I'll take you back now and we'll see that everything's all right."

She made no answer to this, but stayed where he had left her while he put on some boots and a coat. The air outside was quite warm and the night still. Then he took her by the arm and helped her up.

"We'll go back now," he said, and holding her arm they walked back up the path together. There was a light in the house. Rua clung to his arm tightly, but her breathing was quiet and she said nothing. When they got to the house they saw Stenning standing in the doorway in his shirt and trousers, and with bare feet. He did not speak to them. Rua, after hesitating a moment, let go Johnson's arm and ran up the steps; she brushed past Stenning without a word and disappeared into the house. Stenning still said nothing. The light was behind him so that his face was in the shadow. Johnson still waited, uncertain what to do or say, and at last Stenning said: "Good night," speaking quietly and normally, and turned, going into the house, and shut the door behind him. Johnson walked slowly back to his *whare* and, getting into bed again, rolled himself a cigarette. After a while, watching through the open door of the *whare*, he saw the light in the house go out. He finished his night's sleep without being disturbed again.

Nothing was said the next morning when Johnson went into the house for tea before milking. Down in the cow-shed with Rua, he said to her, trying to break the silence which had become worrying to him, half-jokingly:

"You all right, Rua? I thought there was murder being done last night."

Her face was composed and quiet, but her eyes still showed that she had been crying. She gave him a look that was long and sulkily penetrating and said:

"I'm all right."

Then, surprisingly, she smiled at him in a way that was more friendly than anything he had known before.

Out on the hills that day with Stenning, cutting scrub, they rested for lunch in the shade of tall manuka and it seemed to Johnson that Stenning was embarrassed, wanting to say something. Johnson waited, not able to encourage him. At length Stenning cleared his throat. He kicked moodily with his leg in front of him. He said:

"I guess Rua was a bit upset last night."

"She was a bit," Johnson said.

"She's just a kid. You don't want to take any notice of her. She gets wild ideas in her head."

Johnson said nothing.

"You don't want to worry about her. We don't often quarrel. I guess it gets on her nerves being alone here so much. I'm sorry she disturbed you like that. You were needing your sleep, too, I reckon."

"That's all right," Johnson said.

"She's just a kid really. You wouldn't think she wasn't twenty-one yet?"

"I thought she was more than that."

"She's not twenty-one yet. You can't expect them to settle down, not after living the way she has with all that crazy family of hers. It beats me why she won't settle down more all the same. She ought to have children and settle down."

"Doesn't she want to have children?"

"I don't know. Seems not," Stenning said, and relapsed into silence again. He was playing idly with his slasher, digging it into the ground in front of him. After a while, he said:

"You ought to get married you know, Johnson, if you're

settling here. You'll want someone to keep your house if you get settled in across the river there."

Johnson grinned. "I'm not the marrying sort," he said.

"You ought to all the same," Stenning said. "There ain't nothing against it. There's quite a lot for it."

"Who do you think I could marry?" Johnson asked, still smiling.

"Well, there's plenty around. There's Rua's young sister now, she's a nice kid. That'd make company for Rua here."

"I guess it wouldn't work so well with me," Johnson said. "I've always lived alone."

"Sure, I know," Stenning said. "I've lived alone most of my own life, but it ain't so good, not when you're settled in one place and working hard. You want to think that over, now."

"I'll think it over," Johnson said. "I'll think it over all right, but I guess it wouldn't suit me so well."

"Well, think it over," Stenning said, and they stopped talking for the time.

Johnson did not worry very much about Rua. It wasn't his business to worry whether she was happy or not with her husband. It was easy enough, he knew, for two people living continually in that quiet and solitude to get sometimes so that they might want to kill or hurt each other. He did not envy either of them very much in their relations; Stenning, middle-aged and almost ugly, bent with work and engrossed in his farm, or Rua, young and still almost pretty, bored and slovenly and lazy. He did begin to worry when, after that evening's disturbance, Rua began to take a friendly interest in him.

When he first came there she had resented him; after that she had gone on to ignore him. It had been clear enough at first that she did not like his being there. The companionship and the interest that he had there was with Stenning in their work and in the farm. She had a habit whenever they were in the house together of always interrupting Johnson when he spoke. She always helped him last at meal-times, so that it should be plain that he was their servant and not one of them. Johnson remembered how angry she had been when Stenning made the offer to him of a third share in the farm, though she had not dared to speak of it directly to him, and if she argued with Stenning against it her talking had had no effect. If Johnson had asked himself at all, or cared, he would have agreed that she still disliked him and wished him gone.

Now, when she first began to behave friendly towards him, he thought that it was just gratitude for his having helped her when she was frightened. When it went on he reckoned it must be just boredom and devilment and perhaps a line she was working on Stenning. A little later he still reckoned it was only boredom and devilment, but he could see that it might be serious for everybody before she had finished. He himself hadn't ever liked or disliked Rua. He had taken no notice of her except to be irritated sometimes by her noisiness and slovenliness. He disliked dirt, preferring to be clean himself, and in the welter of smells that belonged to the farm, from the reek of stale milk to the greasy smell of wool, he would probably have admitted that Rua had a dirtiness of her own. He was annoyed now to have to take notice of her seriously for the first time.

The new behaviour began with a greater politeness. It went, too, with a tendency to change sometimes in the evenings and to do her hair. Johnson thought this was all for Stenning and guessed Stenning thought so, too. The house was cleaner and tidier than it had ever been. It was a general period of good behaviour. He refused to realise that most of it, and probably all of it, was for him.

February ran into March and March into April. Johnson had
been there a year. In the long days, with the sun still hot and so
much work to do, it was easy for the days to go by and to miss
things that happened gradually. In a company of three people,
to whom an outsider was an event, it was true that personalities
could be magnified until they became unbearable; it was equally
true that they could be drowned in the monotony of continual
intercourse. Johnson and Rua were together milking the cows
for an hour and a half each day. It got to be a habit for Rua
to finish first and to stand beside him talking. After that she
wouldn't hurry to begin separating, but would wait so that they
finished up and walked back together. One day, while he was
separating in the small dairy-house at the side of the sheds, she
came in. He turned to take the bucket from her and emptied it
into the bowl. When he had done so, and had put the bucket
down, she leaned forward suddenly, and, putting one arm round
him, put up her cheek to his. It was an odd gesture, half-loving,
half purely Maori in welcome or greeting. Johnson had not
touched a woman since he left Auckland. He put his arm round
her and kissed her fully on the lips. She stayed there a moment,[37]
then turned and ran out of the dairy. Johnson, feeling no more
than bad-tempered with himself, finished separating, and took
the buckets up to the house.

After that, kissing Rua became a habit. Sometimes he liked
it, sometimes she bored and irritated him, generally he thought
both Rua and her kisses silly. He said to her once:

"You better start and behave yourself, Rua. One of these
days Bill's going to see you doing this and he won't like it." He
used Stenning's Christian name only when speaking of him to
Rua. She laughed, shrugging her shoulders.

37 a moment] for a moment

"He won't see me," she said. "If he does he wouldn't care."

"He'd care all right," Johnson said, but she laughed again. If she had to take Stenning seriously she clearly wasn't prepared to do the same with Johnson.

In mid-April Stenning got a contract with a farmer on the main road to do some metalling in preparation for the winter's mud. The money involved wasn't very great, but it was cash, and would be useful. Cash was a Government commodity with which farmers had otherwise little acquaintance. It was a week's work and for that week Stenning rode off alone down the road for the day. The first day Johnson was out riding along the telephone wire looking for a break. He found it where the branch of a burned and dead tree had taken the single wire and its post to the ground, and spent most of the day repairing it, getting home late in the afternoon. The second day he was at work clearing a small patch of scrub near the house. It was a hot day, more like summer than autumn, and he worked through the morning cutting manuka and laying it so that it would burn when they fired it. The hot sun played on his back as he worked and the morning seemed long. At lunch-time he heard Rua call and was getting ready to go up to the house when he saw her coming across the fields towards him. She had a basket and a tea-billy with her.

"I thought we'd eat down here by the river," she said. "It's hot in the house."

Johnson boiled the billy by the river and they ate there. It was a better lunch than usual. Rua sat beside him on the patch of sand while they ate. It was warm there, but not too warm. The sun had gone farther north; it was not the real summer sun that made shade necessary. The fine river sand was warm and soft, and the river looked cool and green going by. While they ate Rua was in good spirits, making little jokes and laughing at the things that amused her. After they had eaten she put her arms round him and her face up to his and they lay together on the sand.

Johnson felt grateful and kindly towards Rua as he had never felt before. She was good to him there and he felt clean and refreshed. Lying there in the clear sunlight and with the air fresh around them was pleasant; it made him feel stronger and more alive. Rua sat up, smiling down at him. She ran her hand through his hair and laughed softly.

"You've got nice hair, Johnnie," she said. When her voice was gentle and soft like this it was the thing about her which came nearest to being beautiful. After that she bathed in the river while he watched her, swimming across to where it ran deeply under a bank of fern and green moss and back against the stream, coming out to dry herself in the sun. The light brown of her body was very pure and natural looking and attractive with the water glistening on her clean shoulders. Then she came and sat down beside him again. After a time, Johnson said:

"I better go back to work."

"Sure, you better go and get some work done," she said. While he was gathering up the lunch things and packing them in her basket, he said to her:

"You won't be able to do this sort of thing too often, Rua."

She laughed again. She was very cheerful.

"Why not?"

"There'll be trouble," Johnson said, "and trouble's not worth having, not even for you."

"There won't be any trouble," she said. "You see, there won't be any trouble," and then she added, laughing at him, "you better run along and do some work now. I'll take the basket back."

Johnson went back and cut scrub through the afternoon, working heavily with a slasher into manuka that was thick enough to need an axe. He was still working there at five in the afternoon when Stenning came home and rode over the field to him. Johnson stopped work to talk to him.

"That's cleared that all right," Stenning said. "That's a good job done. There's only the little patch by the corner left and we'll have this paddock all in grass. It shouldn't ever have been left so long."

Johnson nodded, leaning on his slasher. Sweat was running down his bare forearms and his face was red and hot with sun.

"The little bit won't take long," he said. "How's the road?"

"It's all right," Stenning said. "We're half done. It's going to be a job to make it last the week," and he grinned. "I'll get the cows in for you," he said, and rode away.

Johnson got his coat and sat down for a moment to roll a cigarette before walking up to the shed. The sun was well down now in the west, but the air was still warm. Taking it all in all, he reckoned this was Rua's day.

There was another fine day of scrub-cutting after that and they had lunch again down by the river, then the last two days of the week were overcast and wet. Johnson worked in the wool-shed, making gates for a new yard, and went to the house for his meals. In those days it was not as good with Rua as it had been on the first day; it was not as good to him again. Rua was happy and more contented than he had ever seen her, but he felt himself sick with her and with what they were doing. It was, he knew, not ever going to be as good again as it had first been, and he did not want it to continue. He did not want trouble. He was not afraid of it, but he did not want it. In the life which he had there now, with Stenning and the farm, he did not want to be disturbed by Rua, who did not matter to him at all. On the Friday, the last day, he said to her:

"I reckon that's the end now, Rua," and he pulled her head down close to him so that he could look at her, saying: "Listen, now, Rua, that was all right, but it's the end of it now, and you and I, we're both going to forget it, see."

She smiled at him, rubbing her cheek against his.

"I won't forget it," she said. He gripped her arm more tightly and was about to say something more to her when she said: "It's all right, Johnnie. I'll behave myself, Johnnie, all right. But I won't forget it," and she smiled again. She had a confidence and a cheerfulness which surprised him.

Chapter **XIII**

It was a relief to get back to work again with Stenning. They were busy for a few days clearing up a few odd jobs near the house and making the yards drier and cleaner for the winter. Rua was quiet and contented. She rode over very happily to see her people on the two Sundays that followed. Johnson, ready to forget what had been between them, felt assured.

A week later he went down with the cream to the corner one morning and, being later than usual, got there just as the cream-lorry came. Johnson waited to talk to Sayers, whom he did not often see. Sayers pulled up the lorry and got down to lift in the cans with Johnson helping him. They exchanged their news and Sayers had got aboard again and had his hand on the gear-lever when he leaned out the window again and said, "Johnson!" He seemed to have difficulty in saying what was on his mind. Johnson waited, watching him curiously.

"Say, Johnson," he began again, wrinkling his brown, bald forehead. "I'd leave Stenning's wife alone, if I were you."

"You'd what?"

"I'd leave Stenning's wife alone if I were you."

"Who the hell says I'm touching Stenning's wife?"

"People around here."

"Does Stenning say so?"

"No, you're lucky, he doesn't. You can bet if anyone says so it's his wife. She can't keep her mouth shut. She likes trouble."

Johnson said angrily: "All I know about it is it isn't true. You can tell that to anyone you like."

Sayers looked at him curiously.

"Listen, Johnson," he said. "I liked you the first time I saw you. You're worth more than Stenning or his wife. I pick up

127

all the gossip on this road, but I don't always talk more than I can help. I don't know whether it's true or not true. Whichever it is, I reckon you ought to watch your step. Sooner or later this story'll get back to Stenning and he can be poisonous and dirty when he's crossed. If that little bitch of a wife of his is talking, it'll get back to Stenning and he won't like it."

Johnson nodded. He had stopped being angry. "I'll watch it. Thanks," he said.

"You can suit yourself," Sayers said. "If it was me I'd try a new farm." He grinned and waved his hand as he let the clutch in. The lorry clattered off in dust and loose metal, and Johnson rode slowly home, trying to argue out with himself the situation in which he was placed. If it was true, and if Rua was talking, it would be better to have a showdown. He could deny it or tell Stenning it was true. Either way, if they talked it out, he could convince Stenning that Rua didn't matter to him, that he didn't want her. He couldn't judge accurately how Stenning would take it. To see Stenning marrying Rua for anything else but a house-keeper and an extra hand with the cows was hard. Stenning at forty-five, ugly, thick-set, and slant-eyed, but remembering Rua, as she was when she was pretty and cleanly dressed and young like her age, it was possible that she had meant and perhaps still meant more to him than that. He got back to the house with the problem unsettled in his mind.

That evening, milking, he tackled Rua about it.

"Sure, no, boy," she said. "I haven't been talking."

"Someone's been talking."

"They always talk like that around here. They probably said it the first day you were here."

Johnson was still angry. He said:

"Someone's been talking and it isn't me. I tell you, Rua,

if you're after trouble around here, you'll get it. You'll get it all right from Bill or from me, or from both of us. That's the truth."

She did not answer and they did not talk any more so that he went back to the house alone afterwards, not sure whether she had been frightened by what he said or not.

The summer broke about then, first of all in a thunderstorm that raged for hours over Ruapehu, black swirling clouds hiding the peaks and blue lightning hovering over the bush below, until the storm moved westward across the country and covered their valley. Heavy rain poured down, soaking the summer dry hills until they ran with water, and the river roared by, muddy and brown. The next day there was a driving wind from the south-west and cold showers. The summer was at an end. Tracks and roads were soft with mud again and the grass that had been brown on the hills turned back to green.

It was just after this that Johnson guessed, for the first time, that the news which Sayers had had must have got round to Stenning. At first he was not sure. Waiting for some sign of the kind, for an explosion or a demand from Stenning, he guessed he might be growing imaginative, taking from every habitual silence or moroseness something that was not in it. But he soon grew to be sure. He did not know who would have dared to tell Stenning, but it came one day after he had ridden into the town to a sale. It might not have been conveyed to him in any direct way, but in a joke or an aside or in something he had overheard. However it had been, Johnson was sure that the suspicion was there.

At first it was just in silences and ill-tempered replies. In Stenning, or in any of them, such things were not unusual. They came now in a form that was disturbing. Johnson and he had never talked more than was necessary; but they had talked

about the farm and the stock and the work that was to do, and
had discussed and argued with equality. Now this had gone.
When Johnson said anything, made any comment, Stenning
sometimes did not answer or spoke shortly. After a day or two
of this Johnson himself stopped talking. Words between any
of them on the farm had been few enough before; they now
fell to nothing. After that Johnson noticed at meals Stenning
watching him and watching Rua.

Johnson said to Rua at milking:

"What's up with Bill?"

"He's all right, ain't he?" she said. "He's just the same as
usual."

"He's not all right. There's something on his mind."

"If there is, he ain't spoken to me."

"There's something wrong," Johnson said.

Just after that Stenning took over the milking himself
so that Johnson had no opportunity to talk to Rua alone.
It seemed to him clear that Stenning was always about and
always came into the house when he himself went in so that
he should never talk to Rua. Johnson tried once or twice to
open up things between Stenning and himself. He said to him
once: "What's on your mind?" and Stenning, not turning to
look at him, said: "Nothing I know of. Is there anything on
yours?" He tried once again and Stenning made no answer, so
he gave it up. He wanted to talk things out with Stenning so
that they could go on again as before. He felt sure himself that
he would never want to touch Rua again, had never wanted to.
But Stenning was too forbidding. You couldn't talk to a man
like that who never looked at you except when he thought you
weren't looking and who never spoke.

It was at the next stage of their relations that Johnson knew
he would have to go, when Stenning started wandering about

in the evenings carrying his gun. The first time Johnson heard him it was late at night and he had been sleeping. He woke up suddenly, thinking he had heard someone at the door of his hut. When he raised himself on his elbow there was no sound, but as he sat there listening, he heard Stenning's footsteps gliding away back towards the house. It was certainly Stenning. No one else could have that same slow, solid, dragging walk. The path between house and *whare* was laid with rough duck-boarding on which footsteps sounded clearly. Johnson waited, sitting up in bed, until the footsteps died away into silence and then afterwards he lay awake for a long time, but heard nothing more. Johnson said to him next morning, as they bailed the first cows for milking:

"Did I hear you about last night?"

"I don't know. Did you?"

"Sure. I thought I heard someone walking past the *whare*."

"That was me then. I was just looking around to see everything was all right."

"There wasn't anything wrong was there?"

"No. There wasn't anything wrong, but I like to make sure."

By good luck Johnson caught Rua for a moment alone that day. Coming back behind Stenning from the hills he found her driving the cows in for them from the paddock. He said:

"What was Bill doing last night?"

He thought that for the first time she looked a little frightened and a little afraid, and was glad of it.

"I don't know," she said. "He didn't say. He just went out."

"He was walking about by the *whare*."

"I don't know. He took his gun out with him."

"He did, did he?" Johnson said. "I don't like it."

"I don't like it much. He's all right, I guess. He hasn't said anything."

"I don't like it a bit," Johnson said. "Seems to me we're all going crazy in this place."

He saw Stenning come out from the house on his way down to the milk-shed and rode on to unsaddle his horse.

The next night nothing disturbed him, but two nights later he heard Stenning again. This time, sleeping more warily, he woke at once when the footsteps were near the house and coming towards him. He got out of bed and threw open the door. He called out: "Who's there?" Stenning's voice came back to him out of the gloom: "It's all right, Johnson. I'm just looking around."

"Is anything wrong?"

"Not yet there isn't. It's all right. You'd better get back to bed."

Johnson could see the white of Stenning's face now, about twenty yards from him. He could not see whether what Rua had said was true and whether Stenning carried his gun. Neither of them moved for a moment and then Johnson went inside, shutting the door behind him. In bed again he heard Stenning walk past the *whare* towards the sheds and then turn and go back again to the house. After that again everything was quiet, but Johnson did not sleep. When he did sleep he did not sleep well.

He woke early in the morning. It was just five o'clock and growing light, and he knew that he would not be able to sleep any longer. He got up and drank some water from a jug that he kept in the *whare*. There would not be tea in the house for another hour. Then he sat on the edge of his bed, wrapping a blanket round his shoulders, for the morning air, now that he had opened the door of the *whare*, was cold and damp; he rolled himself a cigarette. Thinking over the night before and Stenning, he knew that he would have to go. He had been there a year. It was not as long as he had meant to stay, but he would have to go. That's the end of this ride, he said to himself, there's always something, it's hard times or bad luck, or the boss doesn't like you, and now it's this Rua. It's this kid that doesn't care a god-damn and likes excitement and trouble. Me, I don't like trouble, not now, I'm getting older now so I'll have to be moving. And this Bill Stenning, that's no way for a man to go on getting crazy over a thing like that. It's this living alone in the country does it. It's a hell of a thing, you can't live in the towns and in the country they all go crazy. So I'll be moving again.

Smoke rose up from the flat, tin chimney of the house. Someone was making tea. He waited a little longer and then went over to find both Rua and Stenning in the kitchen. Nothing was said then, or later, when he walked down with Stenning to milk. It was a silent war.

Riding home that afternoon Johnson made the effort to say what he had been trying all day to bring out. He called out to Stenning when they came to the last gate into the home paddocks and Stenning turned his horse to wait for him.

"I've been thinking," Johnson said. "I've been thinking I might be leaving."

Stenning sat still on the mare, his head bent, thinking.

"Where for?" he asked.

"Heard some time back," Johnson said easily, "from a friend up north—wants me to join him. If it's all right with you, I'll be doing that."

Stenning put his hand down to open the gate.

"When d'you want to go?" he asked.

"End of the week, I thought. All right?"

Stenning nodded as he pushed open the gate. "All right," he said, and digging his heels into the mare cantered across

the paddock. Johnson stopped to fasten the gate and then rode
more slowly after him. That's a hell of a thing, he thought, and
a way to treat me. That's a hell of a way to end a partnership.
That's the end of this little run that was going to settle me nice
and dry and comfortable on a farm here and marry me off to
one of these girls. That's the end of that all right.

Stenning must have told Rua, for she spoke to him about
it at supper that night when they were both there. She seemed
to be taking it very well, and carrying off her side of the play,
though her voice, when she spoke, was unusually bright and
her great dark eyes full of light.

"You're leaving us?" she asked.

"Yes, I'm going."

"Where you going?"

"I'm going north."

"Whereabouts north?"

"I've a friend just taken over a place near Whangarei—that's
away north. I'm going to join them."

Stenning took no part in the conversation, and as far as
Johnson could see was not looking at them.

"Heard from this fellow some time back," Johnson said,
trying to lie well. "Wasn't thinking of going. But I don't
know—winter coming on, I guess—made me think of it. You
get it cold down here."

"Is it warm up north in winter?"

"Warmer than here—lot of rain, but there isn't no frost or
snow up there."

"What sort of a farm is it you'd be going to?"

"Biggish dairy farm—no sheep."

Suddenly Stenning spoke surprisingly.

"We'll be sorry you're going," he said. He sounded more
friendly than he had been for a long time.

"I'll be sorry, too," Johnson said, playing up to him. "I don't know. I never could stay one place too long. That's been my trouble, I guess."

Stenning pushed his chair back noisily and getting up stood by the fire filling his pipe. His presence there was more dominating than when he had sat silent at the table. The conversation came to an end.

That day was a Wednesday. Johnson sent a message down to the corner to arrange for Sayers to pick him up on the Saturday. This'll amuse Sayers, he said to himself, if it doesn't amuse me. He had no very clear plans, but reckoned he would probably go north again. What he had said had been partly true. It would be good in many ways to get away from the cold and the threat of snow. He would draw from the bank the twelve pounds that he had and go to Auckland, and then on farther north from there.

He and Stenning worked the next two days on the farm as if nothing had happened and as if Johnson were not leaving. Stenning began to talk again about the place as if it still interested Johnson as it had done, and on the last evening Johnson rode home regretfully, feeling the clear air about him and watching the light fade on Ruapehu as he had watched it when he first came. But he knew that there was no way back from where they were now and that he had got to go.

On Friday, Johnson's last evening there, he went early across to the *whare* and packed his things in his kit-bag by candle-light. He was going to walk down to the corner after breakfast the next day. He had never accumulated possessions and so did not have much to take. Some worn-out clothes and a pair of boots, half-gone, he left behind. By nine o'clock he had finished and the little hut looked bare and tidy. After that he got into bed and read for a while before putting the light out.

He had only just gone to sleep when he was woken up by Rua bending over him. The last few nights before this he had locked the door of the *whare*. This night, knowing it to be his last, he had not bothered. He woke up with her warm face against his and her breath in his face. She must have come very quietly. He sat up and put out one arm to hold her.

"You bloody fool," he said angrily. "What in hell are you doing here?"

Rua was not upset. She laughed half to herself and held him tightly with both arms.

"I don't care," she said. "I'm coming with you."

He forced himself out of bed, pushing her back, and finding his matches lit the candle. He wanted to get her back to the house as quickly and quietly as possible. The first match spluttered and went out. The second caught on the wick which flickered a moment and then burnt up. It showed Rua sitting on the edge of the bed; her eyes were very wide and shining. She laughed again softly and leaning across blew the candle out.

"I like the dark," she said, from out of the darkness that followed. Johnson felt in himself an over-burdening anger and irritation, a desire to strike her and hurt her. He put down one hand and closed on her arm, trying to pull her up.

"It's all right," she said. "I've told Bill. I'm coming with you."

"You're not coming with me," he said coldly and angrily.

She twisted herself, wriggling away from him, and the fingers of her other hand laid themselves softly on his bare arm; and like that he felt her fingers stiffen until the nails sunk into his flesh. At the same time he stopped still where he was, for he, too, had heard what she heard, coming along the track; the sound of Stenning's slow dragging footsteps.

Johnson heard Rua gasp with a great intake of breath. She

let go of him and shrank back towards the wall. Johnson knew
that he would get no help from her. She had probably dared
such a situation as this. It was one thing to risk it, another to
encounter it and go through with it. Johnson stayed quite still
hoping that, as it had been before, Stenning would go past the
whare. His footsteps came nearer—it seemed very slowly—and
neither of them moved. Johnson could hear inside the *whare*
Rua's quick frightened breathing, and underneath his feet the
floor was damp and cold. The footsteps stopped outside and
there was still silence, and then the hope that Johnson had went
as he heard Stenning call his name. Stenning's voice sounded
hoarse and unnatural, full of something that was either grief
or pain. He called twice and Johnson did not answer. He
heard Stenning come up the three steps to the door and try the
handle, and he heard Rua's almost inaudible whisper: "I locked
the door." There was a blow as Stenning's great fist smashed
against it, and another as he drew back his foot and kicked it.
The second time he did this the thin wood pulled away from
the lock and the door swung open.

Outside the sky was clear and star-lit and in the first moment
there was a rush of cold air into the room. Johnson could see
Stenning outlined in the doorway. He wore a light shirt which
showed up in the darkness. Johnson hoped that his own khaki
and grey in which he had been sleeping was not so obvious.

Stenning said: "Come on out, Johnson. I want you."
Johnson still did not move. He knew that when he did move
whatever he did must be done quickly. Stenning said again:

"Come on out of there, Johnson."

In the silence that followed Johnson heard a sound that
was familiar to him, the click of a gun being cocked, and
there came, too, a half-smothered cry from Rua as she also
heard it and knew what it meant. The sound that she made

was odd and disheartening and penetrating, like a trapped animal. Stenning stiffened, turning towards her. Doing this carried him sideways on to Johnson who felt his muscles relax in action that was welcome to him. He sprang forward and closed with Stenning. He put one hand on the barrel of the gun that Stenning carried forward across his body and drove the other hard into his stomach. Stenning went back and would have fallen, but came against the side of the door. He grunted, and the pent-up fury that had been in his voice came into his left hand as it swung against the side of Johnson's head. Johnson could not go back. He knew that what he must do was to get Stenning away from his gun and himself outside the *whare*. He still held the gun with one hand, now putting his other hand lower down he tried to twist it from Stenning's hands. They stood for a moment, not fighting each other, but wrestling for the gun, and Johnson, knowing that he might fail in this against the strength of Stenning's forearms, threw himself against the other's body while he fought for it. The first barrel went off, firing between them with a sound that was deafening in the small hut, and that dazed Johnson, so that he fell back, one hand still clinging to the gun. The second barrel went off, as if it had been with the shock of the first shot. It blew its way through Stenning's left shoulder and the side of his head, so that he dropped without a sound and, falling, lay half in and half out the doorway with his head on the floor, his legs hanging outside, and his arms in front of him.

CHAPTER XIV

The silence that fell in the hut after the explosive sound of the two shots had died away was very complete: it had a heavy and final quality. Johnson was dazed by the wind and noise of the shots that had gone so close to him; he felt his face roughened and blackened by them. He put out one hand to steady himself and felt the edge of the plain wood table beside his bed with the candle and matches still on it. Lighting the candle he felt his hand shake uncontrollably. When the flame burned up he could not see for a moment; then he walked unsteadily with the candle across to the doorway to look at Stenning. It was not necessary to look long or closely at him; he was very dead. It was a kind of mockery to think of what lay there as being Stenning, with face and shoulder merged in a mess of blood on the floor. Johnson had not contemplated before the effect of a shot-gun at close quarters; it was like some old memory of the war that he had drowned. He turned and came back, still walking unsteadily, to put the candle down and to sit on the edge of the bed. It was an odd mechanical motion that made his fingers, at this moment, fumble in his pockets for tobacco to roll a cigarette. They met nothing and he remembered then that he had been sleeping in these clothes and that the pockets were empty. His hands dropped listlessly and his eyes wandered again towards Stenning.

Rua had not moved until now from where she had been, huddled up in the far corner of the bed against the wall. She sat up now, leaning forward. The light of the candle was kindly but showed enough. She was quiet for a moment and then broke out, with a voice that was half crying:

"My God," she said, her voice rising, "you've killed him."

"I didn't kill him," Johnson said, without emotion. "He tried to kill me."

She gasped, looking fearfully at the dead body of her husband.

"God," she said, her voice dropping again to a whisper, "God, and he's dead now."

Her hands were clenched and her eyes were staring at Johnson. He moved uneasily.

"He's dead all right," Johnson said. "We can't help that now."

Rua got up as if with difficulty from the bed. She did not look again at what lay on the floor nor directly at Johnson. She said: "You shouldn't ever have come here, you shouldn't have come. I told Bill that."

She shivered at the sound of her dead husband's name. Her voice was thin and high-pitched. Great tears welled into her eyes and while Johnson watched her, curious of what she should say or do, he felt within himself an odd helpless pity for her as for a child.

"That's right now," she said, "that's how it was. But you had to come and stay here, making up to him to get part of his farm and laughing at him all the time, laughing at us both. Laughing at me, yes, you were laughing at me, too, all the time. Well, he's dead now, he's dead, isn't he? That's good enough, ain't it?" and her voice rose until she screamed shrilly.

Johnson caught her arm and held it.

"You can cut that out," he said. "There's no time for that now." She was quiet at once when he spoke to her, but pulled her arm away and stood on the other side of the table from him.

"Can't you go away now?" she said, trying to keep her voice steady. "Can't you get out now, now that he's dead?"

Johnson said, speaking softly and levelly—he was trying to pick his words carefully, but found, nevertheless, his speech blurred and his throat dry as if he had been drinking heavily:

"You and I are in this together, Rua. That's the way it is and you'd better make up your mind to it. What we've got to do now is to think out what we've got to do."

He felt as if he had grown suddenly very tired and as if he were labouring in a dream to explain something of great importance which could not be explained in words. He repeated:

"We've got to think out what's to do, Rua."

"It wasn't me," Rua said suddenly. "He wouldn't ever have hurt me."

"Yes, I know, it was me all right," Johnson said, keeping his eyes on her. "I'm the home-breaker. It's me that will get the trouble. But you've got to tell what happened. I don't mind manslaughter—I'll get something for that. I don't want anyone to start talking about murder." He stopped, then added suddenly and viciously: "You ought to get twenty years yourself. I didn't ask you down here to-night, did I?"

Rua said, as if she had not been listening to him: "I'm going home. They can find me there when they want me."

"You can't run away from here like that," Johnson said.

She kept her face turned away from him. "Why can't I? You can run away if you want to. I'm going home. I'm not running away."

She turned to go, hesitated for a moment at having to pass across Stenning's body, then went quickly across the room and, half jumping, half falling through the doorway, disappeared into the darkness outside. Johnson got up from the bed and called out after her, but she did not stop, and he heard her footsteps running up the track. He did not call again, but sat there listening. Then he leaned over to where his coat hung at the top of the bed and, taking out his tobacco and packet of papers, began to roll a cigarette. He still felt dazed and as if, now that Rua was gone,[38] the room and everything in it were unreal. While he rolled the cigarette he found himself talking and muttering to himself. Stenning should have known better than to act that way, he was saying, and so should I. We were old enough to know better than that. Only when the cigarette was finished and he put it up to his lips to light it did he seem to realize that his lips were moving and he stopped, ashamed of himself. As he lit the cigarette and drew on it his mind cleared and, looking steadily in front of him at the shadows of candle light on the wall, he thought of what he should do; but his lips still moved unconsciously, framing the words as he thought.

The argument that was in his mind was of manslaughter and murder. No one, he was saying to himself, could make this into murder, not even Rua, and however far her story was from the truth. But he knew that he would not stand well when it came to the law and the people who would judge him. Manslaughter, he thought, and maybe it won't be so bad—a few years in something a little worse than an unemployed camp. But I won't stand well, he thought, with the people around here; there'll be no popularity wasted on me.

He sat up straight at this point and his brain seemed to quicken as if it had come alive again. He looked round the room and saw everything clearly, even Stenning and the blood that was on the floor and splashed on walls and ceiling. He saw this now coldly and unemotionally. He weighed in his mind the possibilities of going away and escaping from it all and knew that, if this were possible, it was what he wanted to do.

38 was gone] had gone

Looking at the situation now, clearly and almost impersonally, he knew that though it would be better if he stayed and faced things out it was not what he wanted to do. It would be the end of the things that he wanted for himself. They would have him then, Rua and Stenning and everybody else. They would take him and tie him,[39] probably for years, to work in a prison-camp, perhaps under the shadow of the mountain there, where he had himself seen the convicts road-making in the rain; and he would be older after that, too old to go away or to do anything with himself. They would have finished him then, all right. If he could get away he could keep some things. He could keep one thing that he had had in all the years that he had known this country, and that was a freedom to go and to work and to live where he liked. He knew now, looking back, how the threat of seeming to lose this had driven him from a relief camp. It was driving him much farther now and a colder, more hopeless way, but it was driving him all right.

His cigarette had gone out and instead of relighting it he dropped it into the blue-enamelled candle-stick. The outline of a plan was maturing, clearly and definitely, in his head. As he stood up he heard, through the night, the sound of horse's hoofs galloping up the road. If it was Rua, as he guessed, she hadn't wasted time; and time was important. He had to get somewhere into bush-country before daylight. It would be a while before Rua or her people did anything; it would be morning probably; they would not want to be mixed up in anything if it could be helped; they would take action reluctantly. He looked at his watch; it was still only half-past eleven. He had gone to bed early and less than an hour must have gone by since Stenning had come to the door. He had six

39 take him and tie him] take and tie him

hours of darkness left to him which should be time enough.

He dressed quickly, changing the soft flannel trousers that he was wearing for strong dungarees. Then he tipped his packed kit-bag out on to the floor and packed it again, this time with only a spare shirt and woollen socks and another pair of working boots, iron-studded with nails. He strapped leather leggings over his trouser legs and fastened a scarf round his neck. While he did this—it took no longer than a few minutes—he did not look towards the body that lay a yard from him, nor trouble about the blood that he noticed for the first time on his shirt and arms. When he had finished all this he looked quickly about the hut, then blew out the candle, and with his kit in one hand, stepped carefully over Stenning's body and out into the night.

Outside there was a wind blowing; it was coming from the east. It blew with a steadiness and strength that meant a gale and rain. He did not worry about this now, but went on up to the house. The front door was blowing open and there was no one inside, so that he knew that it was Rua that he had heard on the road. Lighting the oil-lamp on the kitchen table his eye caught for a moment the telephone on the wall and he wondered, without anxiety, if she had stopped first to give the alarm. While he looked at it the bell rang suddenly and startlingly. In the silence of the empty house the sound was shocking, breaking down his newly-found clearness of mind. The bell rang, two long and one short, and again two long and one short—it was not Stenning's ring but that of a neighbour on the line, four miles down the valley. Johnson went over to the 'phone and lifted the receiver gently. The conversation that he heard came through clearly; a telegram was being read out about the sale of a bull. He heard the voice of the woman from the exchange and the long drawl of the farmer at the other end.

After a moment he put the receiver gently back again.

Johnson went into the kitchen and finished the packing of his bag, fitting each article in carefully. He took a great deal of tea and some salt, and about twenty pounds of mixed flour and oatmeal, as much as he reckoned he would be able to carry easily. After that he went into the bedroom and found Stenning's rifle; it was a small and light .22. He had some trouble locating the ammunition for it, but found at last two packets in the drawer of the kitchen table. He knew that some kind of axe would be necessary to him if he were to keep alive and warm in the bush. There was a small chopper in the woodshed at the back. It was blunt, but it was all that he could afford to carry. He took it, fitting it down the side of his bag, and after that he had finished. He did up his kit-bag and swung it on to his shoulder and pulled his hat down over his eyes, knowing that he was ready to go.

Outside again the wind seemed to have grown even stronger. It was not cold but came down the valley shaking the trees and driving clouds across a waning moon. Going down with a bridle in his hand to find Darky he could not see the horses at first, but found them in the end grouped together in a sheltered corner of the field. When he went up to Darky the horse shied, starting away, and though he followed it quietly, talking to it gently, it would not be caught. The horse had always stood for him before and he smiled a little grimly to himself thinking of[40] the scent of blood that was still on him. He went up to Stenning's Jonquil, standing still and white in the darkness. The mare trembled as he put the bridle over her neck, but stood still, and came quietly when he led her to be saddled. It was just on midnight when he rode out from the

40 of] *om. from original*

farm and stopped carefully to close the white gate that led on to the road. Behind him the farm buildings were dark and silent and in front the road was heavy with the shadows of high clay banks. He rode quickly, using the mare's long raking trot and cantering on straight stretches, or, after they had come to the main road with its rough metal, whenever there was a softer clay strip by the side. He made good progress now, riding through the night along roads that he knew well.

He had to go a long way this time to disappear. He had to go where he could not be found for many months, until perhaps men would think him dead or would stop searching for him. This was too small a country for the fugitive. Men in it knew each other too well up and down each part of the island, and the cities were too small to be lost in. It was an easy matter to watch railway stations and ships. He was going instead into bush country, where for a hundred miles no one lived or travelled, where there were no paths nor animals except birds, but only high bush-hills and rivers going down to the sea. He knew that if he was lucky and could live through this, to come out months later away on the far side of the island, he would still need then to have luck with him, but might win, nevertheless, this game that he was playing. It was a gamble that he liked to think of. It would need not courage, but patience and endurance.

He was going over some of these things as he rode on this first night's journey, with his mind still clear and active. He was not thinking now of anything that lay behind him in the farm-house he had left. He met no one during the night nor was he passed by any cars on the road. He went through the darkened streets of the little dairy town that had served them, riding quietly here so that afterwards men would not trace his movements nor remember the time at which he passed too easily, and went on, going towards the railway and the mountain. He was travelling again the road that he had walked when he first came into this country. The mountain range that he wanted, the only hills that were deep enough and lonely enough for his purpose now, lay eastward beyond Ruapehu and across the tussock plains. He was making for the Kaimanawas, the great range that ran southward like a backbone to the island, its ridges grim and bleak and forbidding, the peaks snow covered in winter. He knew it as a lost part[41] of the country and unknown except to odd prospectors who went into it sometimes, believing in gold that might be there.

Making his plans now as he rode he knew that he could not get as far as that before daylight. Morning would find him on the tussock plains that ran from the foot-hills of the Kaimanawas across to the snow ridges of Ruapehu, and the tussock would give him no shelter if men were out searching for him. He decided then to make this first journey in two parts, with shelter during the daylight in between, and so he turned off and took a road that dwindled to a bush-track, leading, he knew, to Ruapehu itself. He reckoned to trust himself to the loneliness of its rocks and snow for the next day.

Day broke mistily as he was riding the last of the ten miles of this bush-track up the mountain-side. It broke with the wind growing stronger, so that he knew there was indeed a bad gale coming on. It blew fine rain across the mountain-side, wrapping him round. The track ran steeply through tall bush at first and then through bush which shrank gradually to stunted shrubs and mountain grass. He followed it up to where the snow-line came down in winter, but it was May now and only the ice of glaciers was left higher up. Mist swirled in the

41 a lost part] *all edns read* lost part

valleys on either side of the ridge he rode, hiding sometimes all
but the track he followed, and sometimes breaking to reveal
glimpses of rock and ice high above him. He was tired now
and sleepy, and the mare went slowly, stumbling in the ruts
of the path. He came out, at length, where the last trees died
away to a hut of corrugated iron, built for mountaineers, and
sheltered in a cleft of the ridge. He had not known of the hut
and was glad to find it there, but it was a shock to him, now
that he had framed himself into a mood of avoiding all men,
to see smoke coming from the flat chimney. But he was not
really troubled and looked gratefully to it for warmth and
food. The hut was five thousand feet above sea-level and cold
was wrapping him round. He rode Jonquil up to the door of
the hut and, throwing his bag to the ground, jumped down.

The two young men that heard him and came to the door
embarrassed Johnson. They were trampers going over the
mountain in the dead season before the snows came, young
men from college, he guessed, in football jerseys and shorts
and striped stockings. They weighed him up gravely while they
followed him into the hut, ready to show respect to anyone
that was familiar with the mountain. Johnson could not hold
this line. He explained himself shortly.

"Wanted to see this mountain," he said. "Never been up
here before. It's damn' cold."

They agreed, and gave him tea and bread and bacon from
their own meal that they were just preparing. The hut was warm
with a good fire and lined with open bunks. They told him
that they were just leaving and going on round the mountain
westward, and asked him if he were thinking of climbing.

"Not far, I reckon," Johnson said, "not far to-day."

"You want to take an ice-axe if you're climbing," one of
them said. "There's nothing but ice up there now and a little

warm rain to make it slippery."

"The rain isn't so warm," Johnson said.

"It's warmer than the ice. If you're going up the track's clear and marked for the first two miles. You want to watch beyond that with this mist about. It'll be cold out to-night if you miss the track."

Johnson nodded. His eyes were heavy with sleeplessness and he wanted to rest. Outside the wind rising drove light mist against the corrugated iron walls of the hut so that it shook and rattled with the force of the growing storm. One of the young men noticed the rifle strapped beside Johnson's pack.

"You shouldn't carry that here," he said. "This is a game preserve."

"I know that," Johnson said. "I'll not be shooting anything here."

After a while the young men left, shouldering heavy rucksacks and, going westward round the mountain, went out of sight in the misty rain. Johnson took Jonquil down to a rough paddock that had been fenced off below the hut. There was feed of a kind there in the coarse mountain grass, though the paddock was bare and shelterless and bleak. When he had done that he dozed for a little while before the smouldering log-fire, to wake with a start about noon. He got up then hastily, thinking it was no longer safe for him to stay, and, with movements that were still sleepy, fastened his pack with straps from the stirrups of the saddle so that he could carry it over his shoulder, and tied the rifle on top of it. He planned now to go eastwards round the mountain, where there was no track, and, when he had passed the eastern ridge, to come down again on the tussock plains. Ten or fifteen miles after that would take him, crossing the coach-road perhaps by night, to the shelter of the Kaimanawas. Before he went he tidied the hut and let down the rail of the paddock so that the mare could go when she wanted. If she went back down the track now it would not matter much. The mare watched him without moving as he went up past the hut and then eastward across the open mountain-side of rock and tussock.

His brain was working clearly again as he moved against the weight of wind and rain, and he knew what was against him. He had heard men talk of how sometimes prisoners broke from the camp across the mountain and took to the bush. Then it was like a game to the prison guards, a game that they usually won. They picketed all the bridges and cross-roads and searched the mountain huts; after that they waited for the rain that always came to drive the fugitives out of the bush to them. He had on his side some food and an ability to last them out, but that was all.

He had a hard day, going these few miles round the mountain-side. He was forced up, higher and higher, in an attempt to avoid the deep, stone valleys that ran between ridges, steep and unpassable,[42] until he was up near the snow-line coming on small patches of snow among the rocks. Up here the mist driving against him was often half sleet and very cold on his face and ungloved hands. He forced his way on, going as well as he could, and trying to keep his general direction by the slope of the ridges, a journey made hard by broken, ice-worn rock and the heavy pack he carried. The weather cleared for a little while in the late afternoon so that he could see the sharp peak they called Girdlestone above him and could get his line before the mist came down again. He made his way down then, judging himself to have come far enough round the mountain, until he found the edge of tussock again. The

42 unpassable] impassable

bush died away here, on this side of the mountain, into small isolated clumps of trees breaking the stone and tussock. When night fell he dug himself into the loose pumice soil and slept with the sound of wind in his ears, and rain, more heavy now, falling over him. It was a cold night, but not unbearable.

He woke to a morning that was just light underneath a sky still black with the storm. The gale had strengthened so that it had reached its height. He knew well from experience the course that it would take. This was the third day of its fury, with heavy rain in the wind now. It would blow like this all day and another night, and rain heavily, with a steady drenching rain, for two days after that, until the wind went round to the west again. He was chilled and wet through and foodless, but the wildness of the weather gave him a chance of escape.

As he went on in the early morning, fearful of losing all direction, but trying to judge the slope of the land as it ran down to the plain, he came to a strange and desolate country. What he saw was a waste of scarred and pitted desert, bare of all growth for long stretches, loose scoria and pumice powdered to sand by years of weathering, and lifting now, as the gale came violently, so that it rose in swirling clouds that wrapped him round and blinded him. Here and there stunted shrubs clung desperately in the shelter of breaks and hummocks in the sand, and the ground was strewn with the charred fragments of old forests wasted by volcanic fire. He had heard men speak of this, too, of the Rangipo desert, the waste area where long before the volcanoes of the mountain had burned and embedded the forests, and the loose volcanic sand, played on by years of driving winds, had given no home for anything to grow. It was a legend-haunted country, dreaded by the Maoris. He could remember them telling him how long ago the first natives of the country had been driven down here by invaders to die and after that there were stories of Maori tribes caught by snow and starved to death in these same deserts. There had been times when the desert held packs of savage and wandering dogs until they, too, died away in that lifeless area, and it was left as barren and desolate as ever. As he went blindly forward, going doggedly, his head down, barely seeing the ground beneath his feet, he came at length to what he knew must be the heart of it all, Onetapu, the place of the shivering sands. And there he seemed to be caught in something that was wild and furious and stronger than himself. The wind came no longer directly against him, but eddying and whirling in gusts of sand and storm so that he could hardly stand or go forward in any direction. The quiet and silence of the mountain-side was gone and in its place came a sighing and moaning of wind and sand as it stirred in the corridors of the desert, more mournful and more frightening than anything human that he had known. He fought this for a long time, both the feeling of terror and the force of the storm, baffled and angry, going sometimes forward or being swayed to left and right, stumbling and falling, going on his hands and knees, until at last he caught the shelter of a pumice bank and stayed there, burrowed into it, with his back against the shelter and the rain and sand blowing over him. He was exhausted and if snow came, he told himself, ready to die. Night fell and no snow came, but only rain and sand. He ate a little raw flour and oatmeal, moistened into a gritty paste in his hands, and did not sleep, stirring uneasily to keep the circulation in his limbs. With the grey of morning[43] the wind died and rain came down heavily and gloomily: the day was dark and remained dark with heavy clouds. There was almost no visibility, but it was possible to go forward now and to strike

43 of morning] of the morning

a rough line against the slight drift of the rain. He went on until he came out of the sand and on to tussock again that seemed by comparison alive and healthy.

About midday he came to the coach-road that crossed the plains. It was a lonely road and little used so that it seemed more strange to him to hear, as he came to it, the sound of a motor. He waited, crouched in a ditch by the side of the road while a service car went by. The two days that he had been alone on the mountain had already made a difference to him so that he watched this car go by with curious and hostile eyes. In the silence, after the sound of the car's running had died away, he crossed the road and went eastward over the plain. There was no need for him to wait for night: it was difficult enough by daylight covering this tussock country, where the appearance of flatness was deceptive and hid great hollows and billowing undulations. With the grey rain falling it was impossible for anyone to see him a quarter of a mile away, and he guessed that if they were after him they would not be searching these barren plains, but waiting by bridges and road-heads for an attempt on his part at food and shelter. He felt strong still and, so long as he was moving and warm, able to turn his back on them.

The clouds lifted a little in the late afternoon and showed him, for the first time, the shadow of the mountain range ahead that was his goal. The steep bush-hills rose up grimly and darkly out of the plain. But they were still farther from him than he had hoped and he spent the night again on the plain with rain still drenching down. He woke this time before it was light, with his limbs shaking and his jaws twitching uncontrollably, his head burning as if with fever. He was frightened then of falling ill, but the feeling went away as he forced himself up and on again, though his head was light; he felt giddy, and the movements of his legs seemed un-coordinated and unreal. He chewed tobacco as he went forward to keep himself from thinking of his hunger and cold.

Later in the morning he came to the edge of the bush and, as the rain ceased and began to dry in rising mist and fog, he stopped to rest. There, in the first edge of the real bush which closed heavy and damp and dripping, he made a fire, breaking open a dead log with his axe to find dry wood inside it. He cut bits of this into thin shavings, the size of match-sticks, with his knife and, lighting them, built the fire up carefully until it would take great sodden branches in its flames. There was a risk in fire so near to roads and humanity, but he was resolved to take it, and could rely still on the mists and haze of the day which the sun was only just breaking through. He made tea first and drank it black and strong, and then cooked a damper of flour and oatmeal which he ate slowly, drying himself all the time as much as he could, and feeling warmth come back into his body. Afterwards he rolled and smoked two cigarettes—extravagantly, for his store of tobacco was small— and then slept a little while by the side of the fire. He stayed there all day, looking out once or twice, but seeing nothing except the yellow plain and the last clouds rolling back from the mountain, and spent the night there as well, putting the fire down when it grew dark so that its pin-point of flame should not attract attention across the plains. He felt better now and slept easily, unmindful even of a sharp shower that rustled the leaves overhead during the night. With morning, the wind was in the west and blowing freshly.

This was real bush that he was going into now, not the mountain-bush of birch-trees that he had seen on Ruapehu, but deep, thick, and matted, great trees going up to the sky, and beneath them a tangle of ferns and bush-lawyer and undergrowth, the ground heavy with layers of rotting leaves and mould. To go forward at all was difficult, held back all the time by twining undergrowth. The air was dark and lifeless; it was rich with the sweet, rotting smell of the bush, and only stray glimpses of light came through the leaves above. He had only a general and limited sense of direction, but followed the path of a bush creek which wound its way through the bottom of the valley into the heart of the range. He was going deep into this, so deep, he told himself, that he might never come out again. Following the creek bed was difficult and exhausting, but gave some hope of progress[44] with its occasional short stretches clear of over-growing trees. As he followed it in, going for five days laboriously forward, making at best not more than eight or ten miles each day, the hills seemed to close round and over him until he felt himself to be farther than anyone could ever follow him, surrounded and drowned in the hills and bush, safe and alone and submerged. He had to climb after that to get over the first heights of the range that ran up six thousand feet high, and he did this after two weeks of journeying, going up again to a country of bare rock and lichen and down again to a great valley beyond that fell steeply two thousand feet. The day that he came down again into bush country, snow fell. It lay heavily on the heights behind him and would stay there, he knew, through the winter months that were on them now. Even lower in the valley it covered the trees and lay in patches on the ground. He decided then, that if he were to endure through the next three months he must have warmth and shelter for himself, and stopped then, when he came to the depths of this great valley, to find it.

44 hope of progress] hopes of progress

CHAPTER XV

Life in the Kaimanawas, while winter lay over them, wasn't dull, it was too uncomfortable to be dull. Later, when he became weak with exposure and lack of food, there came on him a settled apathy which stopped him from feeling the conditions in which he lived, but this was not dullness; it was a sickness against which he had to fight.

He made his home in a small rock shelter which was barely a cave, by the river at the foot of the valley. The sides of the cave dripped with damp, but after a time he plastered them over with mud and lined the floor with wood and dry stones and leaves on top. The cave was a suitable place to camp because, above it, the river curved and made a bar of drift-wood which was good fuel and more likely to burn than anything that he could find in the bush. He tried once cutting into standing white pine for the resined timber that would be inside it, but the task was hopeless with his small axe. Once, after two days of torrential rain, the river flooded and washed into his cave, driving him out with all his possessions and his rifle, to sit wretchedly on the bank above through the night. But he would not give up his cave and, instead, cleared timber and boulders away from the pool above so that the river could not flood again so easily. When the leaves on the floor of his cave had dried again it remained moderately comfortable.

He lived mainly on what birds he could shoot and this often took a great part of the day because of the care with which he used his ammunition. There were about two hundred shells in the two packets which he had brought. He reckoned to use not more than two a day: if he missed he went hungry. He had never been a good shot. With the little .22 it was easy to miss and he would spend long hours stalking wild pigeon or parakeets, or the insolent and more easy bush-hens, to get shots that no one could miss. He had heard that there were deer in this country, certainly there were in the ranges farther south, but he saw no traces of them in the valley where he lived. He tried several times to devise traps for birds to save his ammunition, but without much success. Pigeon was the best food. For variety he experimented with all ways of cooking, from baking them in clay to boiling them whole. It was a thin and monotonous diet. He had used all his flour and oatmeal in the first three weeks of his journey across the range, when he had not stopped to hunt birds. He found himself now hungering, with a desire that he had not dreamed of, for bread or starch food of any kind. He had heard men talk of eating fern-roots, and tried this, but could not find anything that seemed like food. He guessed that someone who really knew the ways of the bush could have found them, but he was unsuccessful himself. The tea that he made in the mornings before he did anything else was his great comfort. He made it strong and black, boiling the same leaves over and over again, and drank it luxuriously. His tobacco, doled out scrupulously, lasted in all six weeks. After a while he ceased to miss it.

Johnson lost all real count of time there in the dark loneliness of the bush. There was sound all the time, of the river running, and birds from early morning to the owls calling at night, but he felt within himself a great solitude, a feeling which had never troubled him before in the long periods of his life that he had spent alone. There was a heaviness of the bush that pressed upon him, and weighed him down, until the sound of his own voice was startling to him.

He watched the moons go by and when the third full moon, from the day when he had left the farm, began to wane, judged it was time for him to move on. Rain and winter lay as heavily on the country as ever. There was still snow upon the heights above and he knew it would be a long time yet before the real spring or summer came. But he knew also that if he were ever going to move it must be now. He had grown thin so that the bones of his hands and arms showed through the flesh, but he was not yet really weak. What he had to fight was a desire never to move from where he was. Arguing with himself, he guessed it was partly fear of the world outside and the troubles that he had to face, and partly the tiredness of semi-starvation that had weakened him. Whatever it was, he found himself now accepting the discomforts that had at first disturbed him and in a way interested him, so that he would sit for hours by the smoking fire outside his cave in dreams that were half sleep, and then even to go and hunt birds was an effort to him. He fought this weakness until he knew that he could only fight it by going on, and, if he could come through, emerging into the world again. When he had decided this he hated leaving the cave. In his weakened condition it was a hard thing to do. Its rough shelter was more comforting to him than most homes had been. He put off the journey, waiting for the rain to break, and when the sky cleared one day was still hesitating until suddenly, in a fury with himself, he got ready his few possessions and began his journey down the valley.

He had little to carry now except his rifle. The clothes he stood in were torn and a rent in one trouser leg had been roughly mended with flax. He had discarded one pair of boots; the pair he wore were rotten with damp. His beard and matted hair had grown dirtily together, and his eyes were sunken and bloodshot with the smoke that he had allowed to fill the cave continually in an effort to warm it. The bones of his body stood out thinly underneath his clothes; the winter had left its mark on him.

He planned now to follow the river down rather than to lose himself in trying to fight a way through the crossed ridges of this range. The river flowed, as near as he could judge, south and east, and would lead him out somewhere in the eastern province of the island, where, he could not tell, and it did not much matter. For what would happen when he had to rejoin the outside world he did not greatly care. What had passed at Stenning's farm seemed to him already to have happened a long time ago. The effort of driving himself to make this journey out of the hills was as much as he could reckon with.

He followed the river down for days that lengthened into weeks. Journeying in the darkness of the bush he could not tell what progress he was making and seldom the direction that he travelled. His only measure was a gradual, insensible broadening of the river from the creek that he had known at the head, to a torrent whose pools were often too deep and difficult for him to cross. Often, when it ran under steep banks, he would have to leave it and fight his way through the undergrowth on its banks, to rejoin it again, guided by the sound of its waters, and go forward over its water-worn stones until in time he came to identify himself with it and its progress with his own.

He shot birds now when he saw them and often at night would find no energy to light fires, particularly when it rained. He would sleep then, taking what shelter he could from trees. He had none of the strength now that he had once had, but depended on a purpose that moved him slowly and painfully forward. He could not afford long rests in case this purpose failed. He came, in this journey, to hate the heavy silence of the bush and the dense obstructions that it offered to him, where before he had welcomed it as a sanctuary. His joy now was in a stretch of river, where it opened out for perhaps as much as fifty yards with a clear sky overhead.

The journey became desperate in the end as the bush-hills wound on endlessly. He wondered if he could be travelling south and not east, going down the entire length of the range. He told himself that the hills must end, but each day showed him a new curve in their line against the sky, and then there came a day on which he met with real disaster. The river dipped down on this day, as it sometimes did, and he followed it, scrambling along on one bank and clinging to trees for support. He stopped, hearing above the noise of the river a deeper roar as of rapids or a waterfall ahead. Trying to see what was in front of him he swung himself up by a small tree that bent and broke with his weight. He fell and hit against a small boulder that rolled over, throwing him into the river, and he was swept down off his balance. The dark mud brown of the river was icy cold and terrifying in its strength. His hands caught desperately at a rock, slipped, and caught again while water poured over and past him. He hung there catching his breath until he found strength enough to pull himself up. Then he jumped for a rock above and got back to the bank again, where a last effort pulled him up, and he sat cold and trembling. He was unhurt, but his rifle had gone; it had been broken from his back when he fell. After a while he worked his way along the bank, hoping for a chance that might allow him to recover it, but the chance was not given, and fifty yards on he stopped, seeing the ground drop away and the river fall over rocks in a fury of yellow foam to deep pools a hundred feet below. Somewhere down there, he guessed, his rifle lay; its loss meant that he would be foodless now.

The incentive for a final effort came from his belief that he must already have come a long way and that a break in the hills could not be long delayed. He left the river now that it had brought him misfortune and struggled up the side of the valley in an effort to see which way the country lay.

It took him a long time, working his way across the steep side of the valley to the east; it fell steeply in places where the ground dropped to the waterfall in the river and at times he had to pull himself up from sapling to sapling, digging his heels in loose clay. Near the top there was a chalk fall which had taken trees with it and so gave him a chance of seeing down the valley. There was no break anywhere that he could see in the sky-line, but only the curve of bush-hills as the valley swung left away from the setting sun. He sat there resting for a time and then, finding a trickle of water by the clay break,[45] made tea, lighting the fire laboriously with one of the last of his small stock of wax-matches. He drank the tea, which was now his only food, and felt it warm and revive him. Then he got up and pressed on to use the last hour of daylight that was in the sky.

He was going desperately now and as hard and as fast as he could, swinging along and jumping from tree trunk to tree trunk on the steep side of the hills in an energy of excitement. He reckoned himself fit for a good two days or perhaps three. He slept well in a carpet of green and springy moss and was up with the first light of early dawn and a waning moon, but the afternoon of the next day found him tired and dispirited. He was exhausted by the effort of forcing his way through this jungle that seemed to grow more and more thickly as he went on. Supple-jack and bush-lawyer caught and tripped him. To go forward at all was an effort, exhausting at any time,

45 clay break] clay bank

but now that he was foodless, doubly so. To have had some opening as a goal in front of him would have made the struggle possible. The continual sightless darkness of the bush was like a nightmare.

To add to his depression there came, in the early afternoon, a thin mist of drizzling rain that blanketed the hills and cut off the rare glimpses of country on which he depended. He plunged on desperately, not daring to stop, and relying on the slope of the valley to guide him. He stopped in the late afternoon and made tea again, building his fire in the shelter of a great tree that had crashed down the hill-side, tearing up its roots and bringing undergrowth and smaller trees down with it for a hundred feet around. As he drank the tea he began to feel that he was finished. The warm tea cleared his head, but could not take away his weariness or his hunger. He sat, feeling the ache in his legs, the torn side of his right foot where the boot had been wrenched away, his face and hands scratched and bleeding. He was wondering whether the few hours that were left of the day were worth further effort and saw then, without emotion, the clouds of mist that filled the valley divide as an eddy of wind caught and trailed them upwards. For a brief moment a watery sun shone through, catching the same endless line of the ridge on the far side of the valley and nothing beyond that he could see. But his eye caught then, what for a moment he could not believe, hidden in trees miles below on the far side of the valley, the tin roof of a hut. He stared at it till he could believe what he saw, then, standing on the tree trunk, checked it rapidly by the line of the sun and the curve of the valley. It was a good five miles away—a day's journey perhaps in that country—just below the ridge on the western side of the valley. It was only plain to him there for a few minutes and then the clouds came down again, covering everything, and, moving up towards him, drove the fine, wet, chilling mist against him. He gathered his tea-billy and pack together and set off.

Night came as he reached the river and he waited till daylight to cross it. He woke weak and tired, but optimistic, for the sky was clear and if no rain came there was less danger of his missing the hut.[46] Thought of food and shelter within reach sustained and encouraged him. But the mood of confidence passed in the first difficulty of crossing the river, which was steep and swift at this point. He crossed it at last and then, lighting a fire, made his last boiling of tea and went on, discarding the few remnants of kit which he had kept and taking only the small axe for help in the bush.

By the early afternoon he knew, with a sick feeling of failure, that he had lost the line which he had set for himself. He had reckoned to strike diagonally up the western side of the valley and to be guided by the ridge at the top from going on past where the hut should be, but the ridge on which he had relied was deceptive, flattening out and dipping again when he had reached it so that it was impossible to keep to it. Also by this time rain was falling again, not just the mist of the previous day, but falling steadily and heavily. He was calm with the coldness of utter exhaustion as he turned back and fought his way down to the river again. He planned to go farther down this time and to strike up below the hut in the certainty that there must be some track running up to it. Two hours went in getting back to the river, and another two in struggling downstream. He was making only slow progress now, forced to long rests while he gathered himself for each new effort. As night came on, with rain still falling and the sky overcast, he

46 his missing the hut] missing the hut

knew that he must turn in now away from the river if he was to make the hut at all. It would be ill fortune if he had not yet come far enough down river, but he could not trust himself to go on after another cold and foodless night in the bush.

He began to go forward up the side of the valley again, often crawling and climbing on hands and knees, while the bush grew dark around him. His head was at first very clear and his senses seemed alert and over-sensitivized so that he could hear each sound from the patter of rain in the leaves to the rustle of small birds. But as time went on he began to talk aloud, arguing softly with himself, murmuring over each obstruction as he came to it. He went on, unable and not caring to stop, until the full pitch blackness of night was really around him and the rain still falling steadily. He planned not to stop consciously, but as he went on he could feel the strength of his resistance to unconsciousness lessening. The sense of reality that he had had began to go from him until he was struggling with ferns and creepers in dreams that succeeded each other.

He stopped suddenly, not realizing what was strange to him, and then, collecting himself, knew that he was in a clearing of some kind, that for the moment there was nothing in front of his groping hands. In the pitch blackness that held the bush he could see only shadows and forms. He stood up and stepped forward, feeling with his arms outstretched until he met the trees again, then back until he had placed them on the other side. He was on a track of some kind. He was too sick and exhausted now to understand all that this meant or to argue whether he should go up or down it. He had planned to come out below the hut so the hut must be somewhere up the track. He began, with the last effort of weariness, to walk up the track, stumbling over roots of trees that ran across it and fearful all the time of wandering off it into the bush again. The line of faintly lighter sky overhead sustained him.

He had not far to go now and came at last to the end of the track where it turned suddenly into a clearing, and he saw the hut. It stood backed against trees, but through them showed clearly a glint of light from its window. Johnson gathered himself together and walked across to the door of the hut. Dropping the small axe which he had carried all this time from his hand he knocked on the door and without waiting threw it open and went inside.

Chapter XVI

There was an old man in the hut, sitting at a table with his back to the open fire. The old man had long white hair which was smoothed carefully, and a white beard stained yellow round his mouth. He wore an open shirt with rolled-up sleeves and sat at the table eating bacon and broad beans with a sheath-knife from a tin plate. He looked up as Johnson stumbled into the room, bringing with him through the door that swung open behind him a blast of cold air and rain.

"Howdy, mate," the old man said. "Come on in. Shut the door."

Johnson did not hear accurately what he said. He stood up, holding himself with both hands on the edge of the table.

"Thanks," he said. "Thanks very much," and, trying to sit down on the box by the table, collapsed so that he missed the box and fell on the floor. The old man came slowly round from his place by the fire and picked him up without a word. He put his hands underneath Johnson's arm-pits and half dragged and carried him to an open bunk against the wall where he laid him. Johnson was only half conscious of this. He had a dim memory of the old man's face bending over his, the white beard and strong lines of the face with hooked, predatory nose, and of being given warm condensed milk to drink. He watched strangely and without feeling the old man taking his clothes and torn boots off his body. He went to sleep after that in complete deadness; but once, turning over in the night, he saw by firelight the old man lying on the floor of the hut asleep.

When Johnson woke up again it was broad daylight. He felt the aches of his body curiously. His clothes were all gone and he was lying naked and comfortable between grey blankets;

his hurt right foot had been roughly bandaged with a coloured handkerchief. The hut was empty and he dozed off again to wake two hours later when the old man came in. The old man came over to his bunk and looked down at him curiously.

"You feeling good?" he asked.

"I'm pretty good," Johnson said.

"You were sleeping well this morning. I didn't wake you, couldn't 'a done, I reckon, if I'd tried. You talk a lot in your sleep, son, don't you, heh?" and he chuckled loudly. "You was talking away good. You been in the bush long?"

"A month or so," Johnson said.

"Get yourself lost, heh?"

"More or less," Johnson said. "I was trying to get across a bit of country, I found it tougher than I expected."

"It's hard country all right," and the old man chuckled again. "You don't want to come in here unless you know where you're going, no, that you don't." He kicked the fire together with his foot. "Reckon you could eat a bit now?"

"I reckon I could."

"I reckon you could do with a bit. There's bacon and beans." He pushed a wire hook over the centre of the fire and hung a pot of beans on it. Then he cut slices of bacon from a large side hanging from the roof and dropped them into the pot so that they rested on top of the beans. Johnson sat up in his bunk.

"My clothes about?" he asked.

"You ain't got no clothes to speak of, son," the old man said, and continued to chuckle. "I hung 'em up outside what there was of 'em." He took a coat and an old pair of trousers from the back of the door. "You better wear these," he said.

Johnson put them on, dressing himself painfully, and sat on the edge of the bunk, wrapping himself round with a blanket until the meal was ready. The air inside the hut was warm and heavy in spite of the rain and wind that could be heard outside, but Johnson felt weak and cold still within himself. He ate a good meal and drank tea afterwards. The old man did not talk while they were eating except to grunt to himself. He smacked his lips noisily while he ate. When he had finished he filled a pipe, cutting tobacco from a black stick. Johnson refused tobacco and, lying down again without apology on the only bunk, went straight to sleep again.

The old man's name was Bill Crawley. He was surprised that Johnson had not heard of him and refused at first to believe him.

"Everybody knows Bill Crawley, I reckon," he said. "Along the Bay and other parts as well. You can't come into this country without hearing of Bill Crawley."

"I didn't come in from the Bay," Johnson said. "I came in from the other side."

"Did you? All the same I should 'a thought you'd 'a heard of old Bill Crawley where you came from. That was a damn fool thing you did just the same. I never heard of anyone doing that, not all the time I been here. How long d'you take over it?"

"About two months," Johnson said.

"It was good going at that, I reckon." Old Bill Crawley sat up suddenly on his wooden box. "Say, son," he said, with the first sign of excitement that Johnson had seen in him, "there ain't anyone looking for you, is there?"

"Looking for me?"

"Ah, search-parties, friends getting anxious and that, heh?"

"Not that I know of," Johnson said. "I didn't tell anyone I was coming in here. I haven't any family in this country."

The old man sat back relieved. "That's good," he said. "Once there was some trampers lost in here and I had no peace at all for three weeks. They never found them either. Two of them

there was, college boys. That's good. We don't need to worry."
He relaxed, drawing at his pipe. "You better stay on till you get
in shape to go out. It's thirty miles to Waite's sheep-run where
the road starts."

"That's fine," Johnson said. "You sure you don't mind? You
got enough food?"

"There's enough for a month or more. I generally make a
trip out for stores in the spring, 'bout October. There's a gun
there, you can do some fancy shooting." He grinned, showing
yellow teeth beneath his drooping white moustache.

"What do you do here?" Johnson asked.

"I don't do much, son. You looking for work?" He chuckled
loudly. "I used to prospect a bit once, it's too far away now.
They found a little gold right away in here once, never saw it
meself. You after gold?"

"I wouldn't know it if I saw it," Johnson said.

"Every now and again there's fellows in here looking for gold.
There's none here, son," the old man said, as if not believing
his assurance. "They used to think there was. You ought to try
down the West Coast. There's gold down there. I been there. It
rains more there than it does here and the bloody sand-flies—
You'd go a long way before you found a dirtier looking bit of
country than up back of the Karamea. I been in New Guinea,
Australia, too. There's no good gold left now, son. They got the
most part of it."

"What d'you live on then up here?" Johnson asked him.

"I got a little money, son, and a pension. It don't cost much
to live up here." He looked at Johnson sardonically. "My
money ain't tucked away under the floor, if that's what you're
thinking. I got it banked. It pays the store's account."

"How long you been in here then?"

"Couldn't say, son, a fair number of years."

"Since the war, eh?"

"The last war?"

"Yeah, the Great War."

"They've all been great wars, son. My father called the war they had in the 'fifties the Great War. It would be about since then though, I reckon. I was living down on the back of Waite's then, riding his fences, me and my old woman."

"You were married, eh?"

"Sure, ain't you married?"

"No, I'm not married."

"Well, I was. Everybody gets married once. She must have died, my old woman, time of the last war and I moved in here. It was quieter like. That's when it would be."

Johnson, in borrowed trousers and boots with his own shirt and coat patched up, moved about comfortably enough for a few days and began to feel well again, though his feet were still bruised and sore and worried him. Old Bill Crawley would go off, as a rule, for most of the day. He walked the hills, sometimes looking for a bird or a wild pig. He took Johnson up some of the small creeks and showed him where he had washed for gold. But most of the time old Bill Crawley seemed to prefer spending his days alone. Johnson rested in the hut and to make himself useful, got water and wood. He piled up a great heap of firewood at the back of the hut. In the evenings Bill Crawley liked Johnson to read to him. He could read himself, but only with great difficulty. He had a store of old magazines and illustrated papers, some of which dated back five or six years, and Johnson went through them for him. He seemed to like having Johnson there, or at least not to mind him, once he had got his own bunk back and Johnson had made up a bed for himself on the floor.

After about three weeks—in late September as near as

Johnson could judge, for the old man kept no calendar—he said one day to Johnson:

"Listen, son, I'll have to make my trip out soon. You're eating me out of beans and flour."

"I'm sorry," Johnson said.

Bill Crawley chuckled. "It's nothing, son, you're welcome. You just made the spring trip come a little earlier, that's all. I can see the bottom of the flour bin and I'm getting short of tobacco now you got the taste for it again. To hell, it doesn't matter, only I'll have to make the trip, that's all. What you say to coming out with me? It'd be a better trip for you."

Johnson looked at him carefully, trying to judge him. It was an evening, after supper, and they were sitting in front of the fire on boxes. Johnson said:

"That'd be fine. I'd better tell you, Bill, I'll be in trouble when I get out there."

"What sort of trouble?"

"Well, see Bill, I killed a man, that's how it is."

Bill Crawley drew on his pipe.

"That's interesting, son," he said. "How d'you come to do that?"

Johnson told him.

"Well, that's certainly interesting," Bill Crawley said. "That's a bloody interesting story, son. I didn't know I was entertaining such a bloody interesting fellow. But you shouldn't 'a got mixed up with married women, not a man your age. It's all right for young fellows, don't know any better. It reminds me, that does, of a fellow I knew in the Solomon Islands—name of'—he stopped and lit his pipe with a burning ember from the fire—'name of Paynter. He got living with native women there—several of them from what I heard tell—found him one morning in a hut with his head missing. That was the Solomon

Islands. Paynter the fellow's name was. English boy. There's always trouble with the natives there. Come to think of it," he added, "best fellow I ever knew was a Maori."

Johnson brought the talk back on to the lines that concerned him.

"Well, you see, Bill," he said, "the way it is."

"Yeah, I see how it is, son. But they won't still be looking for you."

"They'll start looking for me all right once they see me."

"Maybe you're right. You better stay on here."

"I can't do that," Johnson said. "There wouldn't be enough for two of us. I can't eat up all your grub."

"There's a lot of living in the bush if you care to look for it," Bill Crawley said, "but perhaps you're right. You'd get tired anyway after a time here. If you were my age, you'd like it."

"I'll have to get out," Johnson said. "I just want to find the safest way of doing it, that's all."

"It's a pity you're not a better shot," Bill Crawley said. "You could 'a took up bush-ranging—a man with your record. There's a good living there for an able-bodied man with a good horse."

He wasn't joking.

"Son," he said, reminiscently, "I remember in Australy when they got the Kelly gang—those were the men, heh?—when they rounded up Ned Kelly, six of them, and he got two—dressed in chain armour they say he was at the end there."

"Those days are over, I reckon, Bill. They don't stand for gangs like that nowadays."

The old man shook his head. "I don't know, son. What about that fellow in the Wairarapa?"

"Never heard of him."

"Rode around the Wairarapa for days on end with a gun,

broke gaol and all. Fellows out looking for him shot each other by mistake. They didn't shoot him."

"I never heard of him, Bill."

"Well, he did all right for himself. You could make a good living with somewhere to hide in the hills here—and a good horse. That's the trouble with those fellows, they always want to go drinking around towns with women and all. That's how they always get them. You're a steady fellow, I reckon. You could do well for yourself with a good horse in the Bay."

"They wouldn't stand for it now, Bill," Johnson said. "They'd be out after a man with aeroplanes and all sorts once you started that. They wouldn't like it a bit, nobody would."

"Well, then, what you want to do, son?"

"Get out of the country."

"That's a hard thing to do."

"I know it's not easy."

"You're damn right, it's not easy."

There was a long pause in the conversation while Bill Crawley wrinkled his eyes in thought, pulling on his pipe, and Johnson sat staring into the fire.

"I tell you what," Bill Crawley said, at last. "You better let me go down and see what's being said about you, see if they're still looking for you. Then we can see what to do."

"It'd be damn' good of you," Johnson said. "I'd be grateful."

"We'll do that, son. Then we can see."

"You don't mind my staying here?"

"I don't give a damn what you do so long as you don't want my bunk. I built that bunk myself and I'm too old now to sleep on the floor."

Two days later the old man set off on his trip down to the nearest store. It was going to take him two days to reach it given good weather, a day or two there, and another three days back, packing his stores up to the hut with horses which he borrowed for the job and took back afterwards. Johnson loafed around while he was away and read magazines and chopped wood. It never occurred to him to worry about Bill Crawley informing on him, but he found himself nervous with curiosity as the time for the old man's return came near, as to what the outside world was saying of him. The old man got back late one night after Johnson had gone to bed. Johnson helped him unload the stores and feed the horses. After that he cooked him a meal and they sat afterwards smoking. Bill Crawley said to Johnson:

"Son, they think you must be dead."

"How's that?"

"Well, I looked through the papers," Bill Crawley said. "I'd trouble enough finding anything at all about you without making the hell of a lot too much fuss, but they keep the papers for me at the store the way they always do and I looked 'em through. Took me a time I can tell you. I don't read too fast. It seems they wanted to see you all right when you went away, they was looking for you all right. This girl of yours told the story about quarrelling over her, the way you said she would. Then they never found any trace of you after you was on the mountain—on Ruapehu. They reckon maybe you got lost up there. That's what they say. The fellows down at the store didn't know anything about you as near as I could make out."

"That's fair enough," Johnson said.

"It's fair enough as far as it goes. Now you got to clear the country without them waking up to think you ain't dead."

"That's right."

"It ain't easy."

"I'll bet it isn't."

The old man smoked on in silence for a time while Johnson rolled himself a cigarette. He was enjoying, for the first time, real cigarette tobacco that had been brought in for him.

"You know anyone has to do with ships?" Bill Crawley asked him.

"I worked on a ship once," Johnson said, "on a trading scow. That's the only one I know—fellow called Petersen."

"He be any use to you, d'you think, son?"

"He might be," Johnson admitted. "He's retired now though, last I heard of him's some years ago—lived some little place outside Auckland."

"You better go find him," Crawley said. "You want someone knows about ships. If you could get to Austraily, you wouldn't do so bad."

"That's a fact. That's what I'll do," Johnson said. "I better come down with you when you take the horses back."

"All right, son, but there's plenty of food here now if you want to stay."

"I better go."

"Reckon you're right. You got any money?"

"I got two pounds I kept in my tobacco tin."

"You better take some more. I can lend you a pound or two. You want some money in your pocket."

"I'll be all right," Johnson said. He was reluctant to take money from the old man. "I'll get to Auckland all right. After that I'll take my chance. I'd like these clothes of yours."

"You can have them. We can't have you going down naked, son. You don't look so bad in them."

"I don't look so good." They hung all over Johnson like sacks. "I'll change 'em as soon as I can. There's one thing I would like and that's a shave."

"Son, I told you. I don't know what a razor is," Bill Crawley fingered his beard caressingly. "You wait till morning and I'll go over you with the scissors."

He did this next morning before they started on their journey, spending nearly an hour on Johnson. It was slow and painful though he handled the scissors with great care. At the end of it Johnson's hair was a reasonable untrimmed length and his face made him look like that of a man who badly needed a shave. They set off about midday riding the two horses, the pack-saddles padded with sacks to keep them away from the hooks.

"Knew a man got caught on those once," Bill Crawley said, "and travelled three miles before the horse brought him home. A proper case, he was."

Johnson had borrowed an old hat from Crawley and a pair of boots. He knew that he would not feel comfortable or move easily anywhere until he had clothes that came nearer to fitting him. The track ran steadily down-hill through thick bush. It was well made and clear of roots, nor did it have enough traffic ever to have ruts worn in it.

"Surveyors made this fifty year[47] ago," Bill Crawley said. "God knows what for."

In the late afternoon they came out on to an upland of tussock, a little plateau of dry pumice land. There were some cattle feeding on the edge of the bush as they came out; they ran, startled, back into the bush.

"Waite's always has run stock up in here," Crawley said. "It's God's own game mustering 'em. They're wild as rabbits."

They camped on the edge of this upland before it dipped down again. It was a relief to Johnson to feel himself out of the bush country with some open space around him. They built a great fire which roared up, lighting the fringes of trees and scrub for yards around; and hobbled the horses near them. Bill

47 fifty year] fifty years

Crawley cooked bacon and beans over the fire.

"Can't trust anyone else to do it," he said. "Nine times out of ten they burn the bloody bottom out of the pan."

Johnson made tea and collected wood for the night. After they had eaten and before they had slept, the old man was in a reminiscent mood. He talked about times in the 'eighties when he had made money prize-fighting.

"The 'rib-and-jaw-breaker' they called me," he said. "Son, I fought thirty rounds once in Tasmania at a horse-show for ten pounds. There wasn't any money for it out there. It was all for the sport. Not but what the fellows that bet on you wouldn't throw something in. I was jailed once after a fight in Bendigo, yes, son, and they passed beer into the jail till the warders were dead drunk in a line outside the cell and fellows fighting each other right away through the jail."

He chuckled to himself at the recollection and Johnson watched him, the firelight playing on his hooked nose and great head while he bent forward filling his pipe.

"You think times aren't so good now as they were then?" Johnson asked him.

"I don't know, son," the old man said. "I reckon they must be much the same."

"Maybe, you haven't been out much lately to see it," Johnson said, "but times have been hard lately all round."

"Times never was so damn easy," Bill Crawley said. "You should've been in Ireland when I was a boy."

"How old d'you think you are, Bill?"

"I don't know, son," he said. "My old woman could 'a told you. She used to reckon things like that up when she had nothing to do. 'Bout eighty, I reckon. How old are you?"

"I'm thirty-six."

"You're doing right, son, to try and stay out of jail. It's a pity for a man to waste the best years of his life that way. When you're seventy or so it won't matter."

Early the next morning they started down the track again and, going through broken and half-burnt bush country, came to the edge of Waite's farm and the first fence.

"I wouldn't come any farther," Bill Crawley said, "not now with me. We might meet someone. It'll look awkward if they see you walking out o' here with me. They're used to me by meself. I'd lie up here till dark and get out of this hill country before anyone knows where you come from. It's two miles on to Waite's homestead. It's five from there to Wakanui—that's where I'm going. That's where there's a store and a post-office. Past there ten miles you come to a better road. You get out on there, no one won't worry about where you come from."

Johnson nodded. He got down from his horse and fixing a rope on the bridle gave it to Crawley.

"I won't see you if I go through by night," he said.

"That's right," the old man said. "You won't see me. I'll sleep at Wakanui the way I usually do. You'll be all right now. You got some grub for the day?"

Johnson nodded. The old man kicked his heels into the pack-horse he rode and started off.

"So long," he said. "Don't go shooting up too many of your friends when you get out." He turned round to speak over his shoulder. "Don't let them catch you," he said. "It won't do the fellow you shot any good and you'll only be an expense to the Government."

"So long," Johnson said. Bill Crawley turned round once again twenty yards down the track.

"You might drop me a note," he called out. "Let me know how you get on. Wakanui Post Office—I'll pick it up some time."

"I'll do that," Johnson said.

The old man soon disappeared down the track, riding heavily, with his long legs hanging stirrup-less on either side of the pack-horse. Johnson turned off the track into a clump of scrub and settled himself to pass the rest of the day there. He walked twenty miles that night and came out on the main road with cars passing him once or twice. He was conscious once he was out on the road of his loose, ill-fitting clothes and unshaven face. He slept off the road again during the day and went on by night. On the second night he stopped outside a small village. It had about a dozen wooden houses, two stores, a small hotel, and a garage. In the morning, when the bar opened at nine, he went into the hotel.

The owner was as unshaven as Johnson. He breathed frostily of brandy; he was unused to custom so early in the morning. Johnson guessed the drinking was probably done after hours at night. The owner opened a bottle of beer for Johnson gloomily. Johnson tasted it, finding it strange and unpalatable.

Johnson said: "What's this place called?"

"It's Waiapapa," the barman said.

"What's on around here?"

"Nothing I know of." The barman lounged tiredly against the door behind the bar. He looked at Johnson with disfavour. "What d'you expect to find?"

"I don't know," Johnson said. "Any work going?"

"Not that I know of."

Johnson was making himself a cigarette. Lighting it he threw the match into a sawdust-filled spittoon on the floor.

"Got a barber here?" he asked.

"Nope. What you want a barber for?"

"I want a shave."

"Well, there's no barber here."

After a while he spoke again, as if unwillingly. "Ern Thompson at the garage cuts hair sometimes," he said.

Johnson finished his beer and went out. The hotel-keeper watched him go without moving. At the garage he found a boy working underneath a car.

"You Ern Thompson?" he asked him.

"I'm not," the boy told him. "Ern's off on a job."

"When's he coming back?"

"I dunno. Afternoon."

"Can you cut hair?" Johnson asked.

The boy grunted, working away with his head hidden under the car and only his legs showing. "Nope, I can't."

"Can I shave myself here?"

The boy put down his tools and crawled out to look at Johnson. He was not more than fourteen years of age and slightly built with an old-looking face. He looked Johnson over carefully.

"You can go ahead," he said. "The makings are in that little room on the right by the office. I'll have to charge you for that. It'll be sixpence."

"Is there any hot water?"

"Nope, there's no hot water. You got sixpence?"

"Yes, I've got sixpence."

"You better give it to me."

Johnson shaved himself painfully. Staring at himself in the glass he knew that no one would easily recognize him now. The lines of his face had drawn and sharpened with the bush-life and starvation of the winter until they came to a point at his chin. His eyes were deep and sunken and his skin had lost its brown and developed a blue pallor of sunlessness. He looked altogether older. There were streaks of grey for the first time in his hair. While he was shaving the boy came in and watched him. When he had finished he sat for a moment on the running board of the car where the boy was working, and rolled himself a cigarette.

"You going far, mister?" the boy asked.

"Don't know," Johnson said. "Looking for work, just got off a ship down south."

The boy grinned. "Who d'you take them clothes off, mister?" he asked.

"Borrowed them," Johnson said, smiling. "I lost my own."

"Thought maybe they were off that scarecrow Ern had out at the back last year," the boy said and laughed broadly at his joke. He sniggered to himself, going under the car again to work. Johnson finished his cigarette and walked on.

Later in the day he came to a small farm-house set near the road. There were cultivated fields of vegetables behind it and in front of it and in one of these, between the house and the road, there was a woman working. She had her skirt hitched up to her knees and a shawl over her head, and was hoeing energetically along lines of cabbages. Johnson walked up the drive that led to the house and stopped when he came opposite her. He called out to her:

"Got any work, mother?"

The woman rested on her hoe for a minute looking at him, then she bent down again and worked steadily along until she came to the fence where Johnson waited. She put down the hoe and came over to him. She was a middle-aged, flaxen-haired woman with a brown wrinkled face. When she spoke it was with a strong foreign accent.

"What you want work for?" she asked.

"I'd like a meal," Johnson said. "I'd like some clothes if you've got any."

"Where 'r your own clothes?"

"I lost them. I been ship-wrecked."

"You been ship-wrecked?"

"That's right, lost all my outfit in my last ship."

"Well, I don't know," the woman said. "You any good with a hoe?"

"I can do anything," Johnson said.

"I don't mind about that. Can you hoe all right? That's what."

"I can hoe all right," Johnson said.

She regarded him dubiously.

"We might have some clothes about the house," she said. "Some of my boy's. You go around the house to the shed, the little one on the right. You'll find another hoe there. Bring it down here and we'll see what you can do."

Johnson found the hoe and went to work with her. They hoed young cabbage plants, going quickly along the rows, clearing the weeds and piling earth up round them. Johnson, unused to work, found it tiring on his back. He felt bound to try and keep up with the woman, but was not able to do it. She gained a quarter of a row on him regularly. After a time, when he began to grow tired, he would rest a little at the end of each row. Whenever he did this she would look up at him; once she called out to him. When it came to be about two o'clock in the afternoon, as nearly as he could judge the time, he shouted across the field to her:

"Say, mother, you stopping for lunch any time?" She shouted back to him, without putting down her hoe.

"We don't eat before milking time, mister."

They went on working. At the end of the afternoon a youth of about twenty came across from a field on the other side[48] of

48 the other side] the opposite side

the house and stood at the end of their field watching them. The woman stopped at the end of her row and called to Johnson.

"That's enough now. Finish your row, mister." He joined them at the top of the field.

"Fellow wants some clothes," she said, explaining him to her son. The boy looked at him levelly without speaking and they went up to the house and ate eggs and bread and butter and tea. The food was good and Johnson ate as much as he wanted. As far as he could see the woman lived alone with her son, though they did not tell him this nor talk to him while he was eating. Afterwards he helped them milk, and when he came back to the house he found two pairs of old slacks and a coat put out for him on the back-door steps. The clothes were old, though better-fitting than those he was wearing, if a little small. He wrapped them up into a bundle and put them under his arm.

"That's all right," the woman said, watching him. "Don't go getting ship-wrecked again."

She walked round the corner of the house and watched him until he was off the place. He stopped down the road and changed into the new clothes, leaving the old ones behind. He felt better once he had done this, but it rained during the night and he walked, getting wet through, before he found shelter and slept beneath a culvert on the road.

The next day he struck a main road and got two lifts, one into a fair-sized town and another outside it in a road-transport lorry going north. Johnson told the same story of having lost a ship and going north to join another. No one in these inland parts seemed to worry about its general improbability.

"I can take you as far as Hamilton," the driver told him "Don't mind a bit of company on this run. It keeps a man awake."

He took Johnson two hundred miles north through steep bush roads. At one point, before they came down again into the dairy plains that Johnson knew well, he could see away to the south the snow on Ruapehu,[49] standing out against the sky. He felt pleased to be leaving it behind. The lorry was large and built to carry heavy goods; it thundered along at thirty miles an hour over most roads.

"I got a schedule," the driver told Johnson, "two days on the road, a day there, two days back. I get the week-ends at home."

He was a thin, dark, and melancholy man with an Australian accent. Tiredness showed in his voice and face.

They fell to talking about the state of the country. Johnson, now that he was back in civilization, found it hard to accustom himself to conversations in which every man was a politician.

"The country's all right," he told Johnson, "but they're ruining it. That's what they're doing—ruining it. Now take this service. They're running us off the roads."

"Who's doing that?"

"Why, the bloody Government—cuts down the railway traffic, see, so they don't like it."

"Well, that's bad luck," Johnson said. "Was there good money in it?"

"Two-ten a week."

"How many hours?"

"Well, Jesus now, as long as you take to drive. Most of the week."

"Yours a big company?"

"Pretty big. We got twenty of these. Smart fellow runs it, big man in the money, owns a lot of property in the Bay. That's what they do to a fellow here, though. He shows a little

49 on Ruapehu] of Ruapehu

enterprise and they step on him."

"It's a case all right," Johnson said. "It's not a bad country only there's always something wrong with it."

The lorry driver grinned for the first time.

"You got to keep complaining," he said, "otherwise they take no notice of you."

Johnson had a drink with the driver when they got into Hamilton and shook hands with him saying good-bye. He went out into the streets—it was early afternoon—and into a picture show. He came out again about five o'clock. It was still broad daylight. This was a town where he had once known people, only that was years ago, and he felt curiously carefree now strolling down the wide, main street. He walked down to the station and went into a hotel beside it for a drink. He used to come to this place years ago, but there was a new man running it now and he could see no face that was familiar to him in the half-filled bar. It got more crowded towards six o'clock and closing time, and he finished his drink quietly and went out on to the street again. People were coming and going to and from the station, and the pavement was crowded. He stepped out[50] from the side-door of the hotel in front of two Maori girls coming from the station and, looking at them, saw that one of them was Rua.

He saw her first, but she had recognized him before he could turn away. Rua and her companion came to a stop facing him. The woman with Rua was rather older than Rua was; Johnson had never seen her before. They were both well dressed. Rua wore a brown costume, trimmed with pink, and a decorated hat. The expression on Rua's face was one of embarrassment, not of surprise or fear. Johnson, too, did not know what to say.

50 stepped out] turned out

They stood there blocking the pavement, and looked at each other.

"Hello," Johnson said. Rua smiled anxiously. Her cheeks had filled out and she looked fat and well. "What in hell are you doing here?" he asked.

"That's no way to talk to a lady," the older woman said sharply. Rua smiled.

"I'm on holiday," she said. The older woman looked at Johnson, not knowing who he was.

"We thought you was dead," Rua said.

"I'm not dead."

"I didn't really think myself you was dead, but we all thought you was," Rua said.

There was a further silence. People were passing them, going round on both sides as they stood in the centre of the pavement. Johnson began to feel conspicuous.

"I'd like to talk to you a minute, Rua," he said. She glanced at him sideways, rolling her eyes in indecision so that the whites showed. Then she said something to her friend that Johnson could not catch.

"Where d'you want to go?" she asked.[51]

"You can come and eat with me," Johnson said.

"I'll come back to the hotel later," she said to her friend, and she and Johnson went across the road together and into a small fish and egg café.

"You look awful rough," Rua said.

"I'm a working man," said Johnson. He did not take his hat off and was careful to sit with his back to the light.

"You come into money?" he asked.

Rua kept her eyes on her plate. She said:

51 she asked] she said

"Bill left a little money. He was insured, too. They sold up the farm."

"They did, eh?"

"That's right. I come up here with my sister-in-law for a holiday. Where you been?"

"I've been about," Johnson said. "I'm leaving this country. Your sister-in-law know who I am?"

"I don't think so."

"You'd better not tell her. You'd better not tell anyone you saw me. D'you understand?"

"Yes."

"You'd better understand it. You'd better keep your mouth shut this time. If you don't I'll have you in court with me as sure as God."

Rua said nothing.

"You'd better eat that as quick as you can," Johnson said, when they had got some food. "I don't want to be seen about with you."

"Nobody knows me here."

"That's all right so long as they don't. You eat quick all the same."

They did not talk any further while they were eating. There was nothing to say. At the end of it, Johnson asked her:

"Have you got the cash to pay for this? I'm short."

She put half a crown on the table without a word.

"I'll be going," Johnson said. "I'm travelling to-night."

She looked up at him. "Where you going?" she asked.

"Never you mind," he said, and went out leaving her in the café looking after him. He went down the street and back into the town, and took a seat in a service car leaving for Auckland. He felt unsafe and uneasy for the first time.

Chapter XVII

Johnson had some difficulty in finding Petersen at first. He had moved from the little suburb where he had last heard of him as living and gone some miles out towards the coast. Petersen seemed to have paid all his bills before leaving so that no one knew his address and Johnson did not want to make himself too conspicuous in inquiring after him. In the end he waited and asked the postman, who was able to tell him. He walked out then to the coast, following the directions that were given him, and found Petersen's cottage on a point overlooking a deserted bay. It was a trim little white-painted two-roomed cottage with a neat garden and paths paved with shells, and a flag-staff mounted on the little lawn in front. There was no one at home and Johnson sat on the front steps to wait. The first real sunshine of the new summer was warming the hills and sea. From where he sat he could see the islands of the gulf and the trail of smoke from shipping northwards and eastwards coming down to port. The islands near at hand were in grass and green with spring, farther off they went blue into the distance, bush-covered and misty. One or two small boats and a grey-sailed fishing smack close below him were going up towards the port, leaning to the light westerly wind. The wind came from behind him, wrinkling the blue-green water below.

He waited there nearly an hour before he saw Petersen coming up the steep path from the bay. He did not look to have changed at all except that, when he came nearer, his hair and bristled eyebrows seemed to have gone a little whiter. He walked as carefully and solidly as he had always done. His skin was as brown and clear as it had ever been. He recognized Johnson as soon as he came near him. He said:

"Hello, Johnson, what can I do for you?" and without waiting for an answer: "I was hearing of you being in trouble."

"That's right," Johnson said.

"Well, come on in, don't sit out here. The door was open wasn't it? We'll have some tea. I wasn't looking to see you around here."

Johnson followed him in, thinking perhaps the old captain had grown more garrulous from lack of company, but he did not talk while he was moving around poking up the fire in the range and boiling the kettle. The inside of the cottage was as pleasantly dirty and untidy as the cabin on the scow had been and smelled in the same way of fish. Not till they had sat over tea and bread and butter and home-made fish-paste did Petersen ask for his story. Johnson told it without detail.

"Well, I wouldn't ever 'a taken you on my ship," Petersen said, with strong disfavour, "if I'd 'a known you were that kind of fellow, messing around with Maori girls and other men's wives. Didn't you see enough of them up north with me?"

"I've seen enough of them now," Johnson said.

"Well, maybe you never had a chance up north with Tom Blake about. He was smarter than you or me with the girls."

This was funny to Johnson.

"I don't like it," Petersen said, "not you seeing her again. Last night was it?"

"Last night it was. It ought to be all right."

"It probably won't be. One of those two women is bound to talk."

They had their feet up on either side of the stove and Petersen, smoking his pipe, paused to spit accurately into the narrow enclosure of the grate.

"What d'you want now?" he asked.

"I want to get out. I want a berth on a ship."

"It might be done. It isn't easy, not if you're not a union man. It wouldn't be easy at all if they start looking for you."

"They're not looking for me. They think I'm dead."

"You damn nearly were as far as I can see." He smoked on in silence for a time.

Then he said: "Where d'you want to get to?"

"I don't mind—Sydney—San Francisco. Not one of the home lines."

"You're right there. Sydney'd be easiest for you. What you want me to do about it?"

"I thought you might help me to a berth."

"I don't know many of these fellows now. I'm out of things." He re-lit his pipe, then shot a glance sideways at Johnson, straightening out his legs. "I'll see what I can do," he said.

"Thanks."

"Don't thank me. I wouldn't do it for most fellows in your position, only I think you're all right, Johnson. You just made a mistake."

"I made a mistake all right."

"Getting mixed up with a married Maori woman, the hell. Did you go to bed with her?"

"I told you that—yes."

"What was it like?"

"It wasn't anything special."

"It was a hell of a thing to do. You better stay on here and keep out of sight. There ain't many people come around here, but you'd better not be seen."

Johnson spent the early evening helping him coil and rig fishing lines and they went down together to the bay when night came on and laid them at low tide. Petersen went into town the next morning to see what he could do for Johnson. He dressed himself up laboriously and bad-temperedly in his one city suit of navy blue and went to catch a bus. Johnson stayed indoors. There was only one visitor during the day—a baker, who knocked and, when there was no answer, left a loaf on the door-step. It was a wild, squally day. The westerly wind that had been gentle the day before, had risen, and drove gusts of wind with showers of rain against the cottage and down over the bay. Johnson, looking out from the window, saw the waters darken and the horizon of sea and islands shortened with a mist of driving spray. He saw a red-funnelled steamer going out from the harbour and watched it point out to sea; he watched it until the hull and red funnel went down over the horizon and only the trail of its smoke was left as it went out eastwards across the Pacific. He felt caged and unhappy inside the cottage.

Petersen did not come back until early evening. When he came he brought with him another man, who followed him into the back room of the cottage and was not introduced to Johnson. Petersen had an evening paper in his hand which he waved at Johnson. He did not say anything at first, but grunted and scowled, sitting down to take off his boots and easing his feet luxuriously. Then he said, shaking the paper:

"This is bloody fine, Johnson. It says here you been seen again."

Johnson stood looking from one to the other.

"Who's this?" he asked, with a jerk of his head to the stranger. He was a little wrinkled man, not more than sixty, with a sharp pointed beard. He looked at Johnson curiously, as if he were something odd that had not come into his experience before.

"It's all right," Petersen said. "It's Brown, Captain Brown, a friend of mine. I brought him here to see if he could help you. But what about this?" and he shook the paper again.

Johnson took it from him and read the half column that it gave him. It had a photograph of him that he recognized as an old snapshot and a description that sounded oddly unreal, and a report that he had been seen in Hamilton.

He gave the paper back to Petersen.

"It's that Rua's sister-in-law," he said.

"I don't care who it is," the old man was angry. "I don't care which one of your whores gets you into trouble only I don't want any part of it."

"All right," Johnson said. "I'll go. I'll leave to-night."

"You needn't be in such a bloody hurry," Petersen said, and spat on the floor as if ashamedly. "Only the sooner I get you out of this mess and out of the country the better pleased I'll be. Did anyone see you coming here?"

"Not that I know of. I had to ask a postman your address where you lived before."

"Well, you were a bloody fool." Petersen's eyebrows bristled at each turn of his anger. "We'll have to get you out quick," he said.

Brown, all this time, had been studying Johnson with a curious impersonal interest that irritated him. It was as if he were inspecting a murderer that was about to be arrested and hanged. Johnson turned away from them both and got them supper, and after the meal they sat round the table and discussed ways and means. Brown and Petersen ran over the list of ships in port and argued about men on them and approaches that might be worth trying. Johnson himself barely listened to them. He was full of resentment against these two older men and inclined to regard his own chances of escape impersonally.

But he felt something of remorse the next morning when he watched Petersen dressing himself up again to go into town.

He felt, too, the uselessness of apologizing for the trouble he was causing and instead made breakfast for him and spent the day cleaning the house, realizing, as he did it, that Petersen probably would not notice what he did, and if he did notice it, probably wouldn't like it. Petersen came back with Brown again about the same time in the evening.

"I think we got you a ship," Brown said.

"You're in a bloody fine mess," Petersen said, with grim satisfaction. "I think they're watching the wharves for you. You been out to-day?"

"No."

"Well the paper says you've been seen in two different places. There's nothing this country likes better than a good man-hunt."

Johnson said: "What's the berth?"

"On an oil tanker," Brown said. "The *Stamboulos*."

"The what is it?"

"The *Stamboulos*. It's a Greek ship."

"It's an odd name."

"It's an odd ship. It's just a lot of flat-iron plating. You got to get on board to-night. She sails at dawn to-morrow."

They sat round the table as they had on the previous evening and Johnson made tea. Over tea, Petersen said suddenly:

"You got any money, Johnson?"

"You know I haven't. I've just got a few shillings."

"That's awkward," Petersen said. "This Italian wants fifty pounds."

"He's not an Italian," Brown cut in. "He's a Greek."

"He looked like an Italian to me."

"His name's Nikopolos. He's a Greek. I've seen lots of them."

"What's he want fifty pounds for?" Johnson asked. "I'll work my passage, won't I?"

"You'll work your passage all right," Petersen said. "The trouble is we had to tell him you wanted to get out of the country quiet. He'll take fifty pounds to keep his mouth shut."

"Will he keep it shut then?"

"I don't know. He may do."

"Does he know who I am?"

"He doesn't yet. He may guess when he sees you."

"I haven't got fifty pounds anyway," Johnson said.

Petersen looked at Brown as if for guidance. He pushed aside his cup and filled his pipe methodically, paring the black tobacco first with a pocket-knife into the palm of his hand, kneading it about with the fingers of his right hand, and then pressing it firmly into the bowl. When it was alight he turned and spat sideways into the fireplace. Then he said:

"I can lend you fifty pounds if I'll get it back."

"It'll take me a long time to earn fifty pounds these days," Johnson said.

"I want it back. Fifty pounds is a lot of money to me. Haven't you got any family in England would send you fifty pounds if they knew you wanted it bad enough?"

"I've got one brother."

"What's he do?"

"He's got a bicycle shop in Aylesbury."

"Where's Aylesbury?"

"It's in England."

"Has he got fifty pounds?"

"He ought to have. I haven't heard from him for three years."

Brown sat without saying anything, but watching intently. He did not smoke. Petersen leant forward, emphasizing his points with the stem of his pipe. He said:

"You write this brother of yours a letter. You write to him

now. Tell him you're in a bloody mess and you want fifty pounds, and tell him to send it to me. I can't wait for you to earn it. Your brother can wait. Anyway they might catch you and I'd never see it. I can't afford that. So you write the letter now before you leave here."

Brown chuckled. He was watching Johnson all the time. "That's fair enough," he said.

Johnson took the pen and paper that Petersen found for him and sat down at the table to write the letter. It was a long time since he had held a pen and he formed the letters shakily. He had difficulty in remembering his brother's address. He had written three lines of the letter when a thought occurred to him and he looked up to Petersen.

"If I've got to go aboard to-night," he said, "how are you going to get the money?"

"I drew it this afternoon," Petersen said. "I've got it here."

Johnson went on with the letter. When he had finished Petersen read it over and, sealing it up, put it away in his pocket.

"I'll post this myself," he said. "I'm going to sail you up and put you aboard to-night. I don't want you going through the town."

"If you're lucky," Brown said, "you'll be off the Barrier by to-morrow morning. You'll be away out at sea by night."

"These ships all carry wireless," Petersen said sourly. "They got to nowadays."

"Where's this *Stamboulos* going to?" Johnson asked.

"Panama," Brown said.

"That's a hell of a place to go to."

"It ought to suit you," Petersen said. "It's full of coloured women."

"You can get a ship on to the Indies and home," Brown said.

Petersen said: "This Nikopolos had a berth 'cause one of his men died here of typhoid. You got his berth."

"That's nice," Johnson said.

"It's not so bad. It might 'a been smallpox. You won't like this Nikopolos much."

"I don't expect to."

"He's a Greek. He's no good. You better give him twenty-five down and sleep with the rest in your socks till you get ashore somewhere. Then you could hand it to him. You better give him some other name. We didn't tell him one."

"I said you were a fellow had trouble with his wife," Brown said.

"Someone else's wife," Petersen said.

Johnson felt better now that there was a prospect of his getting away near at hand. He felt strength inside himself again. He did not mind what Petersen said.

"I reckon I've got to thank you both," he said.

"It's a pleasure," Brown told him. Petersen said nothing.

After a little while Brown went and at nine o'clock, when the last light had gone from the sky, Johnson and Petersen went down to the boat in the little bay below the house. The fierceness of the westerly had gone with nightfall, but it still came in gusts over the hill and rippled the water along the shore. The tide was low and the boat swung on her moorings close to a point of rock. Johnson waded out feeling the water cold about his legs and thighs, and brought her in. Then they took the sail cover off and ran the sail up and fitted the rudder. When everything was ready Johnson let go the moorings and held the jib across to point the boat's head on the right tack. A gust caught them and swung the boat over and out from the bay.

It was a fifteen-mile sail to the inner harbour and the wharves, close-hauled against the westerly. The little open boat sailed well into the wind with an occasional chopped wave coming over the bow and spraying them. This was after they had got round the first point and were in the more open water and longer reach of the gulf. Petersen sailed with one arm over the tiller and his foot on the main-sheet jammed against the coaming. Johnson, sitting with his feet braced against the centre-board case, pulled his hat down over his head and his coat up round his ears to keep the cold wind out. The salt water dampening him where he had got wet bringing the boat in, or now coming in spray over the bow, was cold and chill, but stronger to him and more freshening than the rain and river water that had chilled his blood through the winter. They sailed on past a shore that was dotted with lights from small groups of houses. Seawards the flash-lights from the islands of the gulf winked at them. Petersen broke the silence that had fallen on him to say:

"I hope all this'll be a lesson to you, son. You weren't a bad deck-hand when I knew you. You ought to settle down now and have a steady job."

"The last fellow told me that got shot," Johnson said.

"You ought to think a bit more about yourself," Petersen said. "A fellow like you could have a place and settle down and do some decent steady work. You could have a good place on a ship if you cared to. If you get back to England now, you better try for something like that. The world's full of too many fellows like you not knowing what to do with themselves and wandering round and agitating for more pay and getting into trouble of all kinds. I seen it happening the last thirty years. It was the war did it or what, I don't know."

"I've worked hard all my life," Johnson said, "and been paid damn all. If fellows like me make more trouble now than they used to it's because they've got more sense."

"That wasn't any reason to go shooting up this man on a farm."

"I didn't shoot him," Johnson said sombrely. "He shot himself. I didn't want to shoot him. I liked him all right. There was a reason why it went like that just the same. I've been thinking about that. It came with working away there on that farm, just the three of us, and no pay. None of us had any pay. You couldn't get away. You couldn't do anything but go on working. I've been thinking about that and the way things were there. It wasn't any life."

"You're not much better than one of these reds," Petersen said, "and God knows why I'm going to all this trouble with you and lending you fifty pounds. But I can't see a man that was in my ship go all to bad like this."

After a while they came to the main harbour, past the shore lights of the suburbs and in between the brightly-lit ferry-boats running from the north head to the shore.[52] They sailed on in sheltered water now with the wind coming quietly to them over dark water, past the breakwater and the yachts moored at anchor, until they came to the wharves.

"I don't know quite where this ship of yours is," Petersen said. "I think I can find it." And he sailed close past the wharf-heads looking around him. Lights reflected on the water made it hard to see, but at last he found what he wanted.

"I'm going to land you on the steps at the head of the wharf," he said, "and push off."

Johnson nodded. He was cold still and uneasy.

"You got the money?"

Johnson nodded. The clock on the ferry buildings struck midnight. Petersen took the little boat in neatly with the sheet

---

52 from the north head to the shore] from North Shore to the town

loose to an iron ladder at the end of the wharf.

"Your ship's down the middle on the far side. You'll find it all right. Push the boat's head out, will you?"

Johnson, one foot and hand on the ladder, pushed her head round, and a gust coming round the end of the wharf caught the sail again. Petersen put the tiller over and as the boom swung across was off into the night without a word. The white sail faded into grey and was lost in the darkness. Johnson climbed up the ladder and at the top of it met a night-watchman looking down at him.

"What's your ship, mate?" he asked.

"The *Stamboulos*."

"You got a wharf card?"

"No, I've been out fishing with my mate the last two hours, that's all."

The night-watchman nodded.

"It's a cold bloody night for early summer," he said. "You catch anything?"

Johnson shook his head.

"You're sailing to-night?"

"To-morrow morning," Johnson said. The night-watchman nodded again and went back to his room against the wharf-shed. Johnson walked down the wharf and found his ship. It was like most oil tankers, built flat and low with no shape. There seemed to be no one about on board her though the gangway was down and deck-lamps lit. He found his way forward and down into the forecastle. There was one man there half hidden in the thick, dimly lit air, lying on a bunk. He was a little undersized man with dark hair falling across his face and a sallow complexion. He raised himself on one elbow to look at Johnson.

"Who are you?" he asked.

"I've just come aboard," Johnson said. "I'm signing on. Where's everybody?"

"Late shore leave," the man said. "They'll be back later. What's you name?"

"Harrison."

"You English?"

"That's right."

The sailor lay down again and shut his eyes as if he had lost interest.

"What bunk can I take?" Johnson asked him. The sailor pointed to a bunk on the lower tier opposite himself.

"That's the one," he said. "It was Ponoli's." He crossed himself sleepily, closing his eyes again. Johnson lay down on the bunk and, unlacing his boots, went to sleep. He slept with his left arm hunched over the breast-pocket that held his money and his right arm crooked under his head. Later in the night he was awakened by a light in his eyes and woke to see a man standing over him with a lantern. This was a big man; he had the same dark hair and swarthy face as the other man Johnson had seen, but he was built massively like a bull. He had bare arms bristling with black hair and thickly matted hair on his chest. He said to Johnson, speaking thickly with broken English:

"Who t'hell are you?"

Johnson cleared his head, looking up at him.

"My name's Harrison. I'm signing on."

"Who t'hell told you so?"

"I fixed it with the Captain, Captain Nikopolos."

"You did, heh?"

"That's right. I fixed it with him."

The big man put the lantern down on the floor and laid his right hand on Johnson's shoulder.

"Well, listen you, Har'son," he said. "That's not your bunk—
no—that your bunk over there"—and he pointed to an upper
bunk on the opposite side. "Now you get out, see. You do what
I say for'd here, see?"

Johnson sat up, pulling his shoulder away from the big
man's grasp. He bent down and picked up his boots and,
taking them, climbed up into his new berth. The big man paid
no more attention to him. He put the lantern down on a table
in the centre of the forecastle and sat down. He took off his
shirt, baring his arms and chest. Then he found a bottle in his
kit and rubbed his chest and arms with oil so that the muscles
glistened, standing out in the lamplight. He was a big man. He
must have weighed fifteen or sixteen stone.

In the late afternoon of the next day the *Stamboulos* was
meeting the first of the ocean swell on the edge of the gulf. She
was where Brown had said she would be, passing the Great
Barrier Island. Southward and to starboard the blue mountain
sides of the long Coromandel Peninsula ran steeply down into
the water. The cliffs of the Barrier island were smooth rock and,
above, hills of straggling bush and half-cleared scrub. The sun,
going down in the west behind them, caught the cliff faces and
the dark blue of deep ocean water below them. The swell came
lazily across the Pacific. It had travelled a long way. It welled
up in great rolls, that were lifting the ship's bow as they came,
going on towards the land. In front the horizon curved round
with the emptiness of sea going into the distance. Up forward,
leaning on the rail, Johnson was watching this. It was the last
of New Zealand that was passing them by. The town and the
small islands of the gulf and the low hills of the mainland were
lost behind in the distance, and the glitter of sun on the waves
and the white track of the screw.

Johnson had found the only other Englishman on board,

the captain's steward and assistant cook. He was a small man, a Cockney, with a white pinched face and ears that stood out sideways from his head. He stood with Johnson now, looking towards the Barrier island.

"There's been two good wrecks on those cliffs there," he said.

Johnson nodded. He had done with talking for the time being.

"That's the last of that," the steward said. "That's the last we'll see of that country for a bit."

Johnson was watching it, not knowing what it felt like now to be leaving it. The hills of the island behind, with their sharp clay breaks and patches of fern, were like the hills on Stenning's farm.

"It's the third trip I made here, mate," the steward said. "I hope it's the last. You lived there long?"

"Not long," Johnson said.

"I don't want to come here again," the steward said. "I had a girl in Auckland I met the first time I was there, the first trip out. I was going to marry this girl and take her home. She was illegitimate, this girl, but she told me all about it. She was all right. We had it all fixed up. I brought her out presents and all, this time, and she took them too. We was going to have dinner last night before the ship sailed, her and a friend of hers and another man and me. There was four of us. I ordered the dinner—at the 'Central'—I ordered it for the four. Then they didn't come. She sent a note to the ship, just a note, that's all. I tried to ring her up and they said she was out. So I went up to the hotel. Bring the dinner in, I said to the waiter. It's ordered for four, he said. This is all there is, I said, send it in. After that I rode around in a taxi. I don't remember. I met some of the fellows from the ship and they brought me back on board."

Johnson had been only half listening.

"It's tough," he said.

"She shouldn't have taken the presents and all, and done that," the captain's steward said.

"No, she shouldn't have done that. You don't want to worry about it," Johnson added. "You want to forget it."

"I'll forget it all right, but she shouldn't have acted that way."

"It wasn't any way for her to treat you," Johnson said.

The captain's steward spat over the side.

"Well, that's that," he said. "If I'm lucky I won't be here again."

"It's not a bad country," Johnson said. "It's not too bad."

"They can keep it," the captain's steward said.

"It's going to be a while before I see it again," Johnson said, "but it's not too bad a country. I've had some good times here."

Someone came up behind them. It was the big man, the Italian bo'sun. He laid his hand heavily on the steward's shoulder.

"Well, how you say," he said, grinning. "You feel the better this morning, eh? How you say, ain't love grand, eh?"

"I'm all right now, Louis," the steward said. "I'm all right to-day."

The Italian pushed with his great hand on the little man's shoulder so that he had to hold himself off from the railings.

"You all work up last night," he said. "You and the women, eh? The trouble is you just a little fellow, no good with the girls." He grinned widely, turning to Johnson.

"You, Har'son," he said. "The old man wants to see you."

"Who wants to see me?"

"The Old Man, the Captain wants to see you." He transferred his hand to Johnson's shoulder. Johnson turned to him. He turned his back on the Barrier hills and the light of the sun on its steep cliffs going by.

"You can keep your hands off me," he said.

The Italian dropped his hand. He grinned at Johnson, disliking him.

"Where do I find the Captain?" Johnson said.

"Listen you, Har'son, you ever been on a ship before?"

"I've been on ships before."

"Well, listen, the old man is on the bridge, see, or else he is in his cabin. You go find him and you don't talk back, see?"

Johnson was in no hurry to see the Captain. He did not want to talk to him now, but he turned and went, going aft towards the bridge with the light of the sun on the water and on the country that was dropping behind them coming into his eyes.

PART TWO

Chapter XVIII

When the European fighting started again in the summer of 1936, just a few manoeuvres in Spain down there in the sunlight and the hot hills, just a little sparring to try out the equipment for bigger and better days, a few shots, a few shells, a few bombs, and nobody's business—when all that started some time ago now, Johnson was working on an English farm. He was working there quietly to pay off the money that he still owed to his brother. He was working there because it was the only work that he understood and he was living quietly and saving ten shillings for Jim from thirty-two shillings each week.

He had changed his name by then and changed himself a good deal from the Johnson of other days. He was not the man who had grown up in England by the Chiltern hills, nor the man who slight, callow, afraid, had served with the light infantry in mud and cold and dirt and death, fighting a war, to him incomprehensible, to the world unnecessary. He was not that Johnson who had liked sun and free country and beer and small race meetings, not that man living free, not caring where he worked, what he did. Nor that other man knowing hardship and fear of the future and death by poverty of old friends.[53] Nor that last man hunted, in a life over which he had no control.

He was a different man now, grown old but still active, strength wiry and reserved, no longer eager but still living,

53 of old friends] as old friends

grey but not beaten, moving impersonally and unquestioning through a world of which he had not yet understanding but which he could accept. He stood for the war and the peace in between and the war to come. He had endurance.

This farm was in Northamptonshire, in the lowlands, where the fen country begins to rise into the hills of Lincolnshire. It lay beside the Great North Road. It was old England and new England. Its grey stone walls and buildings were of the slate grey stone that runs over England from Cornwall through the Cotswolds to die away on these Northamptonshire hills. The old house, with its slate roof and courtyard surrounded by barns and outhouses, stood on a rise, and below them was the mill-house and the foreman's cottage. A small stream that ran down to find its way into the sea was dammed up behind the mill-house and ran through it to turn the millstones that, still creaking, slowly ground rough meal and flour for the farm. Near the house were green fields and a small herd of dairy cows, below on the flats[54] pigs moved in open pens. Beyond that were fields with wheat coming up green from the spring rains, and not yet ripened with the summer sun, and long rows of beet and potatoes hoed cleanly. The first field of potatoes had been ploughed up and men moved in line across the field picking them. It was a poor summer in England in 1936. The mown hay lay in the fields and dried, and was soaked again and turned and dried, and soaked until it lay straggling and wispy, waiting to be stacked.

Across from the farm ran the Great North Road with traffic thundering along it night and day. No horses there, but heavy trucks and motor coaches, and the smart cars of new England, tearing through the country-side. There was a

54 on the flats] in the flats

military aerodrome two miles to the north and all day planes sang overhead like fighting birds.

Poets had moved in this country once, Cowper and John Clare, but few poets moved there now.

They were good fellows on this farm, kind, solid, well-meaning fellows. There was Tom White, drove the tractor and the farm lorry, jealously mechanical, no one else could drive them, short, dark, and strong, with two children. Reg and Alf Barrow tended the horses and drove them in the fields. There was little Wilson, not good for more than a hoeing job, but cheerful, unambitious for specialization; and old Joe the verger, growing old now, called from the safe and ordinary slow-working jobs of the farm only at those times when there was thatching to be done and a stack well covered. Solemn Bill Jessup, the foreman, the best ditcher in Lincoln in his day, so they all said, his right forearm monstrously thick with strength as a result and now not hasty nor driving in his work but leaving men alone to go their way. Below the mill in the beet-fields were the three Irishmen, two old men and one young, who came each year and hoed, working piece-work, and stayed over harvest time. They were quiet, poor, unintelligent men. They did their own cooking and lived apart in an old caravan, not caring for friendship with Englishmen. There was Fred Stuckey who could catch rats with his bare hands when they turned out a barn, skilled with birds and animals, hoping some day for gamekeeper's work on the big estates, and Frank Whiteman, home from factory work in the cotton country, remembering big wages and bad times, but cheerful being home again, doing farm work again that he had not forgotten.

Johnson did not belong easily with these men. They were settled in a way that he was not. He worked with them and talked with them. He liked them, was not worried by them, but he made them uneasy. He could feel this. He was older than they were, he was older than old Joe. He was more worn, more travelled, though he never talked of this. He did not belong there and they knew it.

That July Saturday in 1936 when the fighting began was a warm, wild, blustering day in Northamptonshire. Coming in at midday from hoeing beet, Johnson knocked the mud off his shoes, cleaning his hoe, and leaving it in the shed below the mill. He was leaning up against the stone wall, sheltered from the wind, and rolling a cigarette when Bill Jessup came by.

"Boss wants us to get the hay in up top this after," he said. "You good for that?"

Johnson nodded. "O.K.," he said. "I got no dinner here."

"You better come in and eat with us, then we'll get the engine up. Boss wants us bale[55] it."

He stroked his chin, looking up at the sky, the easy purr of Lincolnshire in his voice.

Johnson ate dinner in the lodge below the mill with Bill Jessup and his wife, his small son and daughter, boiled beef and carrots on the oilskin table-cloth. Afterwards he rested his legs in front of the stove while Bill Jessup's wife cleared away.

When they came out into the sunlight again the warm west wind had blown the clouds away, uncovering a tearing blue sky. A solitary aeroplane hovered overhead, pushing slowly into the wind like a boat making up-stream. They went down to the shed and waited for Tom White.

"Old Tom gets real mad if anyone touches the machine save him," said Bill Jessup. "Likely he thinks no one save him knows how to work it."

After a few minutes he came in on his bicycle from the

55   bale] *all previous edns read* bail

village, his bag of bread and meat and cold tea slung over his shoulder. Together they uncovered and oiled the tractor. Tom started it up and they went across to the field where the boys were already at work with the horse-rakes. Up here, and away from the shelter of the hollow, the wind seemed wilder still. The wind caught the rows of raked air-dry hay and blew them across the field again. They waited then until two more men had come back from dinner and the oldest Irishman came slowly over to join them.

Once the sweep had started bringing in hay in loads to the baler,[56] there were not many intervals for talking or smoking. Johnson worked quietly and economically, forking hay up on to the platform where it was caught and pressed. The wind, coming in gusts, scattered the hay from their forks and from the spread of the sweeps, driving it away from them across the field.

As they worked they could see the crowded week-end traffic of the roads going north. In mid-afternoon there were aeroplanes in the air, crossing and re-crossing in formation low overhead. The men working were not disturbed by them. The roar of the engines droned heavily in with the clattering tractor.

When they stopped at five Tom White passed his bottle of cold tea to Johnson, and they shared bread and meat sandwiches sitting in the shelter of the baler.[57]

The boys got talking of the war just casually as they might talk of anything else. Little Wilson was telling them how he was up in London in the war and an old lady met the train, on a mission she was, to entertain country boys in London on leave, and took him home to tea in the suburbs and fed him

56 baler] *all previous edns read* bailer
57 baler] *all previous edns read* bailer

and put him back on the leave train at night. It was surprising the way things happened in war-time, he said.

Tom White, tilting back his head to finish the cold tea, grunted, listening.

"Ah, war," he said. He was too young to have been in the war. "We'll all be in it this time," he said. "Conscription the first bloody day, you can bet on that."

"Not me," said little Wilson. "Passed out C3 at the end of the last'n, Ah did," and chuckled, pleased to think that none[58] of these things, not even the old lady and her cake, would happen to him again.

And Bill Jessup, looking speculatively across the field, nodded, saying:

"Ay, every b—'ll be in the bloudy army first bloudy day. That's a fact."

It was nearly seven by the time they had finished and staked a tarpaulin over the pile of baled hay. The sun was setting when Johnson walked home down to his lodgings in the village. He had fed the pigs by the homestead with Bill Jessup and led two working horses down to the home field. The week's work was over.

Going out through the farm gates on to the road, he met the owner of the farm driving back from Peterborough. He held the gate open for the car to go through and nodded doing so. Coldly the heavy head, with its red burned face and iron-grey hair and clipped moustache, nodded back. The eyes passed over him without friendliness. Johnson worked there on sufferance, a good farm-hand. He did not touch his hat as he should have done. He was not likely to get the friendly recognition that was extended to men who lived and worked a lifetime there. He

58 none] some

represented a foreign and unknown quantity, something alien among the corn. The eyes that met his were without hostility but without friendliness. Johnson closed the gate carefully after him and went on down the road.

There was a cricket fête in the village that night, tents and music on the village green. Johnson avoided that; he avoided, too, the new roadside inn that had been built to draw custom from the north road and took his beer instead in the 'Carpenter's Arms' beside the church. In its low-ceilinged, smoky rooms there was company. Tom White was down there and little Wilson and Bill Jessup came in after a little time.

Wilson and three others played darts. Johnson sat and drank two pints of mild ale thoughtfully. He was reading in the Leicester paper about the fighting that had broken out in Spain. There was plenty of other news in the paper and he was not taking any account of it. He talked to Tom White.

Tom White was telling him about the future of farming.

"There's other fellows," he was saying, "go off the land into the gravel pits and such, better wages, they say, ah, better wages when it doesn't rain, I say. Ah'm sticking on farm. Ah've seen the way it's been coming with the tractor and all. Ah've said to missus, if Ah stick to 't, a man can get to be important to th' farm. Gets so they need you, drive the lorry, drive the tractor, more and more machinery coming on—boss is awake to 't. Told me so. 'White,' he says, 'I reckon for you for machinery on th' farm.' Ah can drive 'em. There's naught yet Ah can't drive."

Johnson nodded.

"That's right," he said. "Machinery's the thing."

"There'll be no end to 't."

"I've seen a lot of it," Johnson said, "one place and another. Used to milk cows with it once."

"A fellow Stamford way has machine for that. Reckon it don't do cows no good."

"I don't think it hurts them."

"Reckon it doesn't do them no good. It wouldn't be in England you were doing that."

"No, it was in New Zealand, Australia."

"Ah, Australy," Tom White said. "Australy, I've heard a lot of that."

His square dark face was thoughtful.

"Never wanted to go there, did you?"

"No, not Australy. Never wanted to travel much. Ah used to think—funny the things you think when you're a kid—Ah used to think Ah'd like to go to China."

They drank up their beer not talking and Johnson nodded, saying good night as he went out.

Lying in bed that night, still wakeful, gazing up at the whitewashed ceiling of his bedroom, Johnson was trying to work something out. He was trying to work out a restlessness that would not leave him in peace. He was thinking of Tom White and his machines, and Bill Jessup who would live and die there with his wife and his two daughters, maids at the house, growing up and marrying and living and dying there, with Lincoln still a far journey to them, untouched by the cars going by and the aeroplanes overhead. He himself could never live anywhere again. He had tried to live and settle and things had happened to him. Now he could not do that again. He lived now to earn his living, and lying there he was thinking, trying to work out in himself what it was beyond that that he could want. There were memories of men he had known and liked, men, black and clay-stained on New Zealand roads, sweating on steamer decks, paint-blistered, dirty, and lice-ridden in the seamen's camp at Panama, tough, sceptical on

New York docks. There was a desire in him now for a life that would give warmth and meaning to these memories before he grew too old, for a life active, but with good food and good drink, and men moving, making something together.

It was not here in old-new England, not in these dark green lanes, not here in this village of stone and whitewashed timbers, with men, quiet, soft-spoken, and honest. He did not know where it would be, and went to sleep hearing up the main street of the village two girls laughing as they walked home from the fair, and the church tower striking eleven through the warm, windy, summer night.

Chapter XIX

The summer ran by, never settled or hot, but with patches of clear sunshine between quick showers. They got the harvest in working piece-work late hours into the evening. It was early in September that he had a note from Jim, the brother, saying that he must see him; it was urgent, Jim said, it was serious, by God. Johnson laughed reading the scrawled pencil note for, to his brother, Johnson was a fearful man, and Johnson, remembering the week-end when he had gone to see them, the children sent away, Jim's wife pale and mean with dislike of him, the small shop, the texts on the wall, could understand what he felt. To be concerned in Johnson's life was as bad to them as crimes committed—and discovered—in their own right. He guessed he would leave the farm now and go and see Jim in London. He would go to avoid trouble for Jim and perhaps because he was ready for movement himself with the winter coming on and the harvest money in his pocket, and each time I move, he said, I carry less.

So he left the farm in September and went down to London. He had a note from Jim telling where to meet him and walked down the Strand on a warm autumn day and waited outside the Corner House for him. You could have seen him standing there hatless and brown and thin, Johnson going on for forty.

Jim came up by himself and they went in and took a table and ordered tea.

"Mabel and the kids have gone to a picture," Jim said. "I wanted to see you. I'm picking them up in an hour's time."

Johnson nodded. He was watching Jim disinterestedly. It was Jim that was frightened and had a hunted look, not Johnson. He kept looking round as if he didn't want to be seen. He didn't look very much like Johnson's brother. He was the same build only darker. His face had a settled, stolid look except now for the expressions of uneasiness that ran over it. He looked like a man that was comfortable most of the time. He was quietly and neatly dressed. He looked like a man who knew his place.

"What's the trouble?" Johnson said.

Jim, not looking at him and stirring his tea, playing with his teaspoon as if he disliked it, said:

"There was someone round asking about you the other day."

"Who?"

"I don't know. I didn't see him. I was working, Mabel saw him. She thinks it was the police."

"Didn't say he was the police, did he? The police always say if it's them."

"I don't know. Mabel was pretty mad about it."

Johnson grinned.

"I'm sorry she was upset," he said. "What did this fellow want?"

"Just wanted to know if we'd heard from you at all. She said we hadn't. He said it was just a routine inquiry. Mabel was pretty upset about it."

Jim was watching the waitress uneasily. He lowered his voice while he was speaking.

Johnson poured himself some more tea. He opened a packet of cigarettes, offered Jim one, and took one himself.

"I don't think they're on to anything," he said. "They wouldn't look for me in this country. I got American papers in Panama, they wouldn't ever pick me up here."

Jim said suddenly:

"You shouldn't've come to see us."

"Maybe," Johnson said. "I wanted to explain about the

money. No one knew who I was."

"Mabel and I've been talking it over," Jim said, still not looking at Johnson. "We think you'd be better out of the country."

"It's as safe here as anywhere."

"It's not so safe for us. We'd be dragged in if they knew about the money, so'd your friend Petersen be. You don't want to get everyone[59] into a mess. It's the kids we're thinking of."

"They're nice kids," Johnson said. "I still owe you some money."

"It doesn't matter about that."

"How much is it now?"

"You've paid me twenty-six."

"I better pay you the rest before I go."

"It doesn't matter about that. We'd be happier if we knew you were away somewhere."

"O.K.," Johnson said. "You don't worry about me any more. You haven't heard from me. I won't write to you."

"It's the kids we're thinking of," Jim said.

"I'll fade away," Johnson said. "I'm used to it now."

Jim nodded. He looked to be easier in his mind. He smoothed down his coat and put a shilling on the table.

"If you'll settle this," he said, "I'll be getting along now."

"Your hour's not up yet," Johnson said, "you'll be too early."

"Got one or two things to do first," Jim said. "I'll be getting along."

Johnson nodded. "O.K.," he said. "You might leave me that paper. I'll stay on here a bit."

Jim put the paper on the table as he got up to go and Johnson spread it out.

59 everyone] anyone

"Things getting warm down in Spain and places," he said, looking at the headlines, but Jim had gone. He lit himself another cigarette and smoked it while he read the paper through.

He didn't leave London just at once. He took a room near Liverpool Street and got work washing cars in a garage. Hell, he said, so long as Jim doesn't know where I am that'll stop him worrying. He liked London. It was pleasant to wander about among so many people. There were so many people that no one cared for individuals. It was as lonely and impersonal as living in the bush. He liked the sailors who drifted in and out of the boarding-house where he lived. He watched them drinking, spending their money, going off again and talked to them, liking them, feeling with them the same feeling of belonging to the whole world and to no one place.

He found he didn't want very much now for himself. He didn't want to drink except modestly, to smoke a little, read the papers, lie in bed Sunday morning. The hours of work were long and the pay small and the air bad, but the work itself was simple.

He found himself wanting to talk more, he was friendly to the men he met, especially the older men. He made friends with a little nuggetty Irishman who was head mechanic in the garage. This little man called O'Reilly gave him easy jobs and didn't worry him.

He tried to teach Johnson something about cars, but Johnson wouldn't learn.

"I'm too old," he said.

"It's dull work just washing 'em down," O'Reilly said. "Me, I could be getting bigger money in one of the big factories, Morris, Wolseley, Vauxhall, there's money there, but hell, that's no life, that's what I always say. You get interested in patching up cars, the job gets you."

"Too old for me to learn now," Johnson said. "This suits me fine."

O'Reilly took Johnson home with him to his house in the suburbs. He was a widower with two daughters who worked in shops and kept house for him, and he and Johnson used to sit in the evenings over a bottle or two of stout and talk.

Johnson told O'Reilly bits of what he had done and O'Reilly had stories of America, where he had worked as a boy, and Ireland in the years just after the war.

"That's one thing they didn't get me in," he said. "There was plenty of fighting back home in Ireland or out Detroit way with the union. There wasn't any need to get into these organized wars."

Johnson told him about Stenning and Rua.

"Me," O'Reilly said, "I wouldn't 'a gone to all that trouble running away. I'd take a term in jail any day. I wouldn't 'a lived that life in the bush, not if they wanted to hang me."

He couldn't understand Stenning.

"If my old woman had done a thing like that," he said, "I'd 'a taken it out of her; she was a good old girl, she never did anything like that, but what's the use going around fighting all the men that get off with your wife if she's fool enough to let them. There's trouble enough about for a man without quarrelling over women."

O'Reilly was interested in politics. He was a Labour and a Union man. He had fought through a steel strike in Detroit and with the I.R.A. and down at the docks in the great strike of 'twenty-six. He had a phrase he liked using, industrial war. He used it a lot.

"It's the only kind of war a man knows what he's fighting for," he said.

Johnson listened, tried to argue with him, was interested, but knew nothing.

"I've never thought things over that way, Jack," he said. "I've just knocked around."

"You've been knocked around, that's what you've done."

"I had some good years."

"Yeah, and you had some bad years, that's what does it, the fellows like you not ever stopping to think, just bumming about, when things are good not a care in the world and when they're bad it's nobody's fault."

"You go ahead, Jack," said Johnson. "You go ahead. I'll listen to the theories. All my life I've been listening to fellows with theories. I don't mind listening to yours."

"This is the solid stuff you're getting now, boy," O'Reilly said. "It's this way . . . ."

Johnson was happy then working with Jack O'Reilly. He got to know a lot of the fellows knocking about the town doing one thing and another. He was happy, not caring, they can't do anything more to me, he said, and he liked seeing these men he got to know trying to do things, like things, be political. Everything that was restless, fighting in them, made him feel good. He even went about with O'Reilly distributing pamphlets, but he gave it up after a while.

"It's embarrassing," he said.

"You don't want to get embarrassed by a lot of smug bastards that don't know what's going on in the world."

"Well, I get embarrassed, I don't know anything myself. Someone asks me what's this for, what's all this about, someone asks me am I a Communist, I say no, I'm a democrat and something about the rights of the working man. It doesn't go down the way it ought to."

Once he got arrested fighting in the East End when the

Fascists were doing some marching. The police crowded in and broke the demonstration and the counter-demonstration up. Someone knocked Johnson from behind with a loaded stick and the next thing he knew he was in a police van being taken to the station. He didn't like that much for a moment, not being quite so close to the police, but he kept quiet and it came out all right.

"He seems a quiet, decent sort of fellow," the police-sergeant said. "We haven't seen him around before," and they bound him over to keep the peace.

"You better not start fighting around too much," Jack O'Reilly said, "they'll go to work and get something on you. They're hell on earth once they want to get a man."

So Johnson kept quiet at meetings after that. You could have seen him standing in the background sometimes, a little shy and out of place, while someone was talking, but quite happy to be there. He went about with Jack O'Reilly and had a drink occasionally with the others and listened to them talking and arguing, not saying much himself.

"I don't know a damn thing about it, Jack," he said.

"You'll learn," Jack O'Reilly said.

"It's security the working class wants," said someone else another time.

"I could do with a bit of that," Johnson said. "I could do with a bit of that all right. There hasn't been much of that about in my time."

"But it's all right," he said once, when they were talking, "I like you fellows and I believe you mean what you say you believe. I'll stay around. I'll even walk in a procession."

But he wasn't in London by May Day.

Early in the New Year, when Jack O'Reilly said he was going to Spain, Johnson said he would go too. O'Reilly was glad though he tried to persuade him against it.

"It's all right just knocking about here," he said. "You come along because you like us, you haven't got anything to do, but this is different. This is war. You get killed in war-time."

"They can't kill me," Johnson said. "I've been in wars, there's nothing in them. The peace is more dangerous."

"You think it over a bit."

"You tell me what you're going for, Jack, then I'll think it over."

"Well, me," O'Reilly said, "the wife's dead and the girls are grown up so it doesn't matter."

"I haven't got a wife," Johnson said. "I haven't got any girls. I'll come if you're going."

He patted him on the back affectionately.

"I like you, Jack," he said. "I like the fellows you go around with. If you're going that suits me."

"You got to fight fascism," Jack O'Reilly said, "wherever it is."

"Sure, I know. Spain or here, you got to fight it."

"You know as well as I do," O'Reilly said, "you know well enough what it's all about."

"Sure, we'll go out and burn some churches and rape some nuns," said Johnson, grinning.

"It's O.K., Jack," he said. "I know which side I'm on."

"It's better than the London winter," he said.

"My brother'll be pleased," he said, later in the evening. "He won't know, but if he did know he'd be very pleased. So'll Mabel, she'll be very pleased."

He had a little of the same trouble when he was interviewed for the brigade.

"I'm not a Communist," he said, "I'm a democrat."

"You're a New Zealander?"

"I've been in New Zealand."

"We had a New Zealand airman who had your complaint. He was quite a good airman."

"He's O.K.," said Jack O'Reilly, who was with him.

"You're not too old for this?" they asked him.

"I'm just starting," Johnson said. "This is nothing."

When he passed the medical examination they took him without any more questions.

Volunteers were banned by that time so that they left together with ten others one Saturday night from Victoria on week-end tickets. There was quite a party down to see them off with the police looking stolidly on, trying to pick up faces from the crowd. In the carriage going down to Newhaven Johnson was feeling happy. He was trying to explain this to a man with a university accent and a bearded face. He was a medical student who was going out with them.

"I've only felt like this sometimes," he said, "going somewhere with people I liked, doing something together. It's a fine feeling. Most of the time a man spends too much alone."

"Did you get this in the war—the Great War—" the man asked him, "marching off together?"

"Maybe, I don't know," Johnson said. "It was a long time ago. I was young then. I was frightened a good deal of the time."

"E viva the government socialista of New Zealand," said a little Cockney opposite that Johnson knew. This was just after a Labour Government got into power in New Zealand, so they were giving Johnson credit for it.

"E viva the New Zealand socialista," said someone else. They were under the illusion that they were going to speak Spanish in Spain.

"They're not Socialists, those fellows," Johnson said,

deprecatingly. "They're currency reformers."

"E viva anyway," said the little Cockney. They were all feeling very happy with the drinks of people that had been seeing them off.

"A man spends too much time alone," Johnson said to himself.

It wasn't so warm or so cheerful when the channel boat got out from Newhaven. Johnson walked round the little bit of steerage deck talking to O'Reilly. After a while O'Reilly was sick and went to lie down and Johnson walked round alone, watching the ship's lights on the waves and the gleam of foam and after a while the lights of Dieppe coming up ahead. He had a drink just before they got in and felt comfortable though sleepy by the time they got into the train. It was more tiring than cheerful though the journey in the train and the wooden benches, cold and tiring too the long journey south after Paris. It was cold and wet the night they went over the frontier. The man who was guiding them lost his way in the wind and rain and they had to wait over night until the dawn broke.

"This is nothing," Johnson said, not cheerfully, but as a matter of fact.

"You bloody democrat," O'Reilly said.

The sun came out for a moment as they were coming down the mountain-side into Spain.

It was the late summer of 1937 when I met Johnson. He was at Jarama before that and afterwards at Brunete. He was at Teruel and on the Ebro. He was at Calaceite and on the Aragon front. I tried to get news of him from people who were there, but few people knew of him.

Someone told me who had met him that he was well and only once wounded, in the arm.

"The boys like him," they said. "He's a good fellow." He didn't want to rise in the army or give orders, they said, but he was a good man. He took what was coming.

He was still in Spain when they started to ship the International Column out and he was caught with others in the great retreat from Catalonia when the German artillery came through. The last word I had of him was from someone who was with him waiting in a tunnel by Port-Bou to get over the frontier. This man hadn't known Johnson, but was beside him, and just caught his name. He was sitting there with them, very cold and hungry, and not knowing what in hell would happen next with the aeroplanes overhead and the roads jammed with half a million people outside. He didn't say anything, this man said. He didn't seem worried or unhappy. He was just sitting there. This fellow guessed he came through alive, but he didn't see him again. Myself, he said, looking back and considering quietly a war that was not very satisfactory, all things quietly considered, myself I find one satisfaction knowing Johnson is still alive. There are some men, this fellow said, you can't kill.